Before the Snow Falls

A story about love, drugs, and living while dying.

By Michael James

1
Ryan

The junkies down on the street have been leaning against windows and graffiti since a few minutes past a quarter after eight. Which is fine, you know? It's just what we do, shoot love and lean on things. From up here, there's a view of Alcatraz and the Golden Gate over the quiet rooftops, and seeing the pair, all hopeful and dumb as shit, makes me want to skip hanging out on the corner and maybe go sell my last painting by the bay.

"Hey," says a new roommate.

"Hi, there."

I adjust in the curved window seat to get a closer look at the fuzzy shins poking out of her dress.

"I like your socks," I say.

"Funny. You didn't overdose, did you?" she asks with concerned eyes.

I shake my head.

"There's still hope, though."

"What's out the window?"

"My friends," I say as I take a pack of cigarettes from my pocket. "Are you a grant kid or a drug dealer?"

"Why do you assume I'm either?" she asks.

"Nobody else moves in here."

"Seattle Arts Grant," she confesses.

"Cool. We could use more drug dealers, though." I lean back, tug on the rip in the side of my blue Chuck Taylors and grab my lighter, knocking the charred spoon to the floor. "So, Seattle, huh? I'm from the Seattle of the Northeast."

"Where's that?"

"Maine."

"I don't think they're very similar."

"No? Aren't they both just metaphors for suicide?"

"I guess. I don't know," she says while leaning against the door frame. "Are you here on a grant, too?"

"No. I'm just here. I'm rich, you know?"

"Really?"

"No."

She crosses her arms and snaps a glare at the Hustler centerfold taped to the wall.

"I take it you haven't met Candy?"

"They warned me about junkie assholes, but I didn't think they were serious."

"Language, please Jaqueline. Children are running around."

"Yeah, crack babies."

"They deserve love, too."

She leaves the living room and goes into the hallway. I light a cigarette and laugh as the bulb above her blows, which is fine because it's fucking daytime, anyway.

"The needle's still in your arm, junky," she says while slamming her room's cracked door.

"My name's not Junky. It's Ryan," I holler, then look out the window while a gay bum couple strolls by, holding hands and passing a bottle.

I rub my eyes then rip out the needle, feeling the skin rise as the dried blood tumbles down the tattoos on my forearm.

"Why are you messing with her, Ryan?"

"Hey, Zeus. I didn't see you over there."

"I've been meditating, and don't say my name like that," he says while unfolding two twig legs in a haze of smoggy sunlight. "I watched you nod off. Are you sure you're okay?"

"You're a real Mexican Buddha, aye, Jesus?"

"This isn't about me. You should stop chasing the dragon. Aren't you afraid of dying too young?" he asks.

"Am I not ripe enough?"

"I'd keep you around for a day or two longer in a paper bag," he says as he pushes up from the floor, walks across the living room, and puts his lips on the top of my head. "I have to go on my alms walk now. Take care."

That guy. I tell you. I only met him two days ago.

"One more thing," he says. "The landlord stopped by while you were cold. He said he's kicking you out."

"Again?"

"I offered to pay your rent, but he wouldn't take it. Even the new girl offered. Sorry, man."

"Great. I'll have to get ahold of Nicole," I say, turning to look out the window.

"Tell Nicole hello for me."

"You've never met her," I remind him.

"Her photo's the only thing in your wallet."

"Why were you in there?"

"Window shopping."

"A real Buddhist, you are, Jesus."

"It was nice knowing you, Ryan. So long."

The tapping of sandals on hardwood disappears down the unlit hallway. Two minutes later, eight stories and twenty-two inches below, Jesus walks in a carless street. His mind points up at the sun behind the smog. He's probably counting breaths from clean lungs breathing dirty air and thinking how profound the whole thing is, like he's shared a wafer with his namesake, and He told him all kinds of cool stuff, the same things he could've learned way easier with an armload of junk.

Claire

The air's cold on the top of Apple Ridge, much chillier than Georgia was. It carries on its hidden currents a bouquet of warm, flowery nostalgia, incapable of being explained any other way than to say it smells like wild lily of the valley and feels like that moment while swimming in a mountain pond when the body's temperature becomes indistinguishable from the water's.

While up here on the summit, the tree's leaves below are mostly green, and a mile away, the Atlantic Ocean is black and broody. I pull into downward facing dog and peak over the cliff. There's a hollow below, a vast green pasture in the center of the forest that cradles my home and the abandoned farmhouse. Toto is next to me, growling at a chipmunk as I shake the hair from my shoulders so the morning sun can warm them as it ignites the foliage that's just begun to die and, as a result, become absolutely beautiful.

I move the yoga mat so it's closer to the cliff's edge. Kneeling, I pull into a handstand. The edge is only a few feet away, while the drop down nears a thousand. Many times I've wondered what it would be like to slip on a pebble and fall, rolling, crashing until finally being delivered to the edge of my back lawn.

I set my feet down then hang my legs over, and see a pair of chickadees preening each other on a stunted tree no taller than my terrier. Toto sits next to me, rests his chin on my thigh, and we watch the birds together.

"Let's go, little man," I say, as the birds flutter away. I roll up the yoga mat, grab the half-drunk tumbler of kale juice and run down the mountain with Toto. He passes me, disappears then reappears where the trail forks to go to River Pond. He stamps his front paws on a mossy rock, barks, puffs out his chest then sprints off on his adventure down the mountain.

Thirty minutes later and I'm off Apple Ridge, running through the field and up the hill to my home where Toto sits, panting in the shade of the porch roof. I rub his head on my way through the front door and go upstairs to the bathroom, toss my clothes in the hamper and turn on the water. I pour in strawberry soap then lay in the cold porcelain tub, allowing the rising warm water to lift my calves until my pink toenails press through the bubbles. I turn the water off with my toes, lean back, and close my eyes.

Once I've finally dozed off, Toto barks. I get out of the tub, dry off, wrap a towel around my hair, pull another under my arms and run, almost falling as my wet feet slip on the wooden stairs. Once at the bottom, I go into the living room, peek through the curtains and see Mom's Prius next to my Subaru. The door handle wiggles, but the door doesn't open. Mom moved in a month ago and still hasn't figured out the door. She knocks, and I wrap my hand around the cold brass doorknob and focus on the "ting" as my two bracelets hit it. I unravel the towel from my head and drape it on the banister behind me, shivering as a freezing droplet runs the length of my clavicle before rolling down my chest and soaking into the towel.

"Claire? Hello?" she calls. "Open this damn door. It's stuck again."

I twist the knob, thump the bottom with my foot and open it.

"Claire!" she says.

"Mom!" I say.

"Step aside, honey. It's cold out here."

"It's a long way from Georgia."

I close the door behind her, and we embrace. Her cheeks are chilled fleece, and mine are warm ice cream.

"Claire, you're so hot."

"I just got out of the bath," I explain.

She steps back and checks me out.

"Nice tits," she says. "I'm glad you take after your mother."

"Mom!" I say, blushing.

"Oh, whatever. If I were in my twenties, I'd let it hang out, too."

"I'm hardly letting it hang out. You smell like pot," I counter and grab her hands. "Mom," I say, leaning in so my forehead rests on her forehead. "Mom, I'm twenty-seven, closer to thirty."

8

"I know, sweetie. But you don't look a minute over twenty-two." She steps back, still holding my hands.

"Sometimes I feel eighty-two."

"You look healthy," she says, her eyes wide, beautiful-blue and bloodshot.

"Thanks, Mom." I laugh and then let slip, "It's the cancer diet."

"Oh, Claire," she says.

A tear falls, and I take it from her cheek with the edge of my thumb.

"Mom, I missed you. Even if you were only gone an hour," I say.

"Ditto," she says, releasing me and hanging up her coat so I don't see her cry. "The Ocean Side guy stopped me again at the end of Ruby Lane."

"Did you tell him we still haven't found them?"

"I did," she says, walks to the kitchen table and takes out her glass pipe. "They're disgusting people."

"Want to play a game of bridge?" I ask while sitting across from her and grabbing the deck of cards.

"Did you want to put some clothes on first?"

"No, I'm good."

3
Ryan

I've just finished packing my only bag, but I'm not ready to leave. There's something sentimental with this shitty room. It's small, half the size of my bedroom I had growing up, but it's become an interactive piece of art. Decades ago, probably when the Sex Pistols and Paula Abdul were still touring, these walls became a canvas for drunken marker art. There are a few *for a good time call*s written, probably from before AIDS killed everyone who ever wrote that. I drew a picture of the Golden Gate on the ceiling last time I stayed here, but now it's hidden in a thick blue marker fog. This room was probably once colorful when the writing was new and still meant something, but what's left is mostly fading ink. I sit on my dresser, looking out the window and consider the breadth of what's about to come.

I trace a crack down the crumbling brick wall next door all the way to the alley, push the syringe's magic button, hold, slide out the needle while the blood's still wet, grab my last bag of h and put the paraphernalia in my hoodie's pocket, pull down my sleeve, pick up my duffel bag, go to the busted tape deck, take the Jesus Lizard cassette my old friend Dave gave me (it might save someone's life someday) and dump the bag of heroin on the floor (the shit doesn't help me paint anymore), light a cigarette, grab my very last painting, walk out the door and, once again, leave my life behind.

4
Claire

"Yes, Adrienne?" I say as I close the book on Prufrock and step away from the podium.

"Ms.-"

"What did I say about calling me that?" I ask.

She blushes and wipes the blond hair from her forehead.

"Claire," she smiles, her silver braces shining the sun. "We're all going to miss you."

"Yeah," says one, then another.

A tear blankets my eye then falls, swelling as it crests my cheek.

"We'll miss you so much. I was super scared to come here, to the University, but my first class with you last year made it so easy."

"I'm happy to hear that. It's been my greatest challenge making English Comp enjoyable."

Jeremiah, who always sits in the back, oddly quiet for having a neck tattoo and, if I may say, quite good looking, comes to the front.

"We got this for you," he says without a smile and hands me a book. "It's a first edition Bell Jar."

"I love it," I say.

By the time I lift my eyes from the first page, Jeremiah's already in his seat, his oily hair back in front of his handsome face.

"I don't know what to say."

"Cliche," Calls Robby from the front row.

"Oh no," I say, go to the whiteboard, pick up a purple marker and write five times, *I will not use a cliche*. "Penance paid." I look at the clock above the door. "I must be on my way."

"Class has been over for a while," Jen says.

"I know. I've got an appointment I don't want to go to." I don't mention it's a surprise visit to the nurse's office. "They may be able to fix me, and I'm not quite ready for the bad news, so I've kept you wonderful children hostage."

"Children?" says Robby. "We could have gone to the same high school."

I smile, wipe my eyes.

"Not quite, Robbie, but thanks just the same."

"Do you want a tissue?" Lila offers from the second row.

"Thanks," I say and walk to her. "I think I may need a tourniquet, though."

"Not to steal your thunder, Ms. Claire, but I'm going to miss Toto so much," says Will.

Beside the podium sleeps my little dog, who's conked out on a fleece pillow Mom made for him. Will gets up from his seat and pets the sleeping beauty, which wakes him. Toto shoots an exaggerated yawn, finishes with a squeal then sets one paw on top of the other and inspects the room.

"Thank you all so much. I'll miss all of you, really."

I grab the full bottle of kale juice from the podium, step into my sandals and wave as I walk beneath the Reaper's mistletoe, which now reads 8:22 p.m.

"Toto doesn't want to leave," says Will.

"I know. I know. I don't want to leave, either. Come here, old man," I say as I stand in the doorway and pet my thigh. My bracelets jingle and Toto's ears shoot up. "Goodbye, my friends."

In the hallway, there's only me, Toto, and the custodian, who's bent, drinking from the fountain.

"Goodbye, Jerry," I say as we pass.

"We'll be thinking about you, Claire. Take care, now. You too, pup," he says with eyes that have been forced in the many decades of his life to accept loss matter-of-factly, no matter how insignificant.

Jerry grabs the mop handle with both hands, it's feathered head in a bucket of soapy water, and pushes the contraption past me and down the hallway, the uneven wheels slapping the tile with each rotation.

5
Claire

I slam my horn and lock the brakes as an eighteen-wheeler cuts me off.

"Ocean Side assholes," Mom says as the monstrous red truck tails away down Route 1.

"I know, right?"

"Anyway, check this one out, honey." Mom pulls out a photo from one of Gram's yellowed envelopes. "That's you and the neighbor kid from when we visited here twenty-something years ago."

"Weird. I think I remember," I say. "You might want to wait to show me those until we stop."

"Probably for the best. You two were so precious, though, your noses yellow from sniffing buttercups. Here's one of both of you on a tire swing. Too cute. I remember that morning."

"Maybe I remember. He has dark hair, right?"

"He does, and handsome eyes."

"Mom," I say with a smile.

"Fine. I'll be quiet," she says as I notice the thousand-page book in her purse.

"When are you going to find time to read Anna Karenina tonight?"

"You never know. A room filled with old people we've never met, my thoughts may drift."

14

"That's why I love you."

"That's the reason?"

"Yep."

"You're so weird."

Three blueberry fields and an alpaca farm later, I pull into the Grange Hall.

"The tide's so low," says Mom as she points behind the old, square building to the half-moon beach of muck in the harbor.

"Let's go out on the dock before everyone gets here," I say as Mom and I hurry down.

"Real quick, though. We've got to get back to help out."

Once at the dock, we don't go all the way out, but halfway, and look down over the railing as black waves turn seaweed into demon hair.

"Do you think anyone would mind if I light a joint?" she asks.

"I doubt it."

Back on the shore, four silent men are bent, digging in the mud as the sun leaves them behind. "It's a great evening for digging clams, though."

"Let's get back," Mom says while taking one last drag before snuffing out the joint.

"Okay."

"Maybe we can find out how to get ahold of that family from one of the locals," she says, "and maybe the cute boy."

"He's my age now, Mom. Hardly a boy."

"And you're a little girl to me, too."

Once we're back at the car, Mom takes the casserole from the Subaru. A truck pulls into the u-shaped driveway and parks next to us.

"You must be Mary," I say to the old lady getting out from the passenger's seat. "Here, let me help you."

"Happy birthday," Mom and I say at the same time.

"Ninety-two years young," she says.

"And you must be Bob?" asks Mom as the driver hobbles around the front of the truck.

"Oh, not too bad for an old fart," he says without hearing her and takes the casserole from Mom. "Here, I'll trade my wife for this."

Mom and I hook an arm through Mary's and escort her up the stairs.

"Well, I remember you from that painting class you taught," she says to me. "Are you one of the volunteers?" Mary asks Mom. "I haven't seen you around. Heck, you could be my son for all these eyes are worth."

"I'm here to help and meet some new people from this wonderful town," Mom explains.

"She just moved into Gram's old house with me on Ruby Lane," I say.

"Cassy's house? Sad about her passing, too young," she says.

I want to say Gram was seventy-six, almost a vegetable for the last decade, and that that's a perfectly normal age to pass, but I don't because Mary's saddened, thinking what a tragedy it is that this child, at seventy-six, has died.

"During the prime of her life, too," I say.

16

"Cut it out," whispers Mom with a smile.

Bob goes ahead, opens the front door, and we catch the dance floor slumbering in the amber-golden light as Mary points to a place just in front of the stage.

"I was born right there, right in the middle." She sets her purse on a foldout table, sits in a cold, gray chair and catches her breath. "They were having a dance, celebrating some anniversary, or something. Maybe it was a Friday night. When I grew up, we always had dances on Fridays. It must have come from somewhere. Anyway, Mother had to come for whatever reason, cook something, help out, dance, who knows? Then there I was. She told everybody I was the easiest birth she ever had." Mary clasps her hands on the table and swells her chest. "Right there, ninety-two years ago. It smells the same now as it did when I was growing up, just like wood stain and seaweed."

"Happy birthday Grammy," says a man with a white beard and red suspenders who's just come through the door.

"Let's start getting ready, honey. We've got to make sure these happy people are fed and have plenty of coffee," says Mom.

"Oh, we love our coffee," Mary claims. "Claire knows that."

"We'll be back soon," I say and follow Mom to the kitchen in the basement.

An hour later and the hall is filled. As strange as it is, taking care of Gram over the years, I've seen many of these people around town but never spoken with them outside of the few classes I've taught here.

"Claire," says Mom.

"Mom," I say.

She grabs my hand under the table and squeezes it.

"This lovely lady sitting next to me, Grace, remembers a few things about the people that lived next to Gram. You know, the boy from the pictures," she says with a wink.

I pull my chair forward and look across Mom to the feeble pink-haired lady named Grace.

"Nice to meet you. I'm Claire. Can you tell me how to get ahold of them? The Ocean Side Farm across the road wants to buy the property, but they can't figure out how to contact them."

"What an' hell they want that for?"

"They want to expand," I say.

"It's a mountain. Expand again? Greedy sons-a-bitches," she says. "Life was much better in Cherryfield before them."

"Mom doesn't like them either."

"What about you, honey?" she asks. "You think they're worth a dollar?"

"I believe they fit into Cherryfield about as good as a stripper," I say, building on her analogy.

"Used to be a real nice farm, the Ocean Side place, back when Scotty Nerson owned it before the Lord took him."

"That's so sad," says Mom.

"Sure is, dear. So, what would you like to know?"

"What can you tell us about the owners?" I ask. "How to speak with them."

"Sure, sure," she says. "The boy's your only chance. Used to have a lot of charm, that house. It's still in there, though, I'm sure of it. Something like that doesn't just get up and leave and never come back. I've got an eye for these things. The Alexanders owned it. I can tell you all about them, but most of it's word-of-mouth. They didn't talk to too many people and what got around wasn't too flattering."

"I don't want to trouble you, just how to contact them is enough."

"Well, as I told you, you'll only be able to find the boy," Mary says as she takes a bite of cold apple pie, wipes her waxy lips with a dirty napkin and continues. "Sad, sad story about the Alexanders," she begins, "crazier than a barn full of owls. Didn't Cass ever tell you about them?"

"She didn't say much. We only visited a couple times, and by the time I came to Maine, Gram was sick, and they were gone."

"When Claire was growing up, we had a hard time leaving Georgia to come visit," Mom explains.

"Single mom, and a little child," I say.

"Well, it's good you're here now." She takes a sip of coffee. "So, about the Alexanders. I can't say what's true and what isn't, and I can't remember the little boy's name, but maybe it'll come back to me once the wine comes out."

6

Ryan

"Twenty dollars and a blow job, maybe."

"Sir, the sticker on the painting has twenty-two dollars and eighty-two cents on it."

"Well, I don't have high hopes for you," I explain as he stuffs a vanilla cone in his mouth.

"It'll be perfect in my office," he mentions and extends a twenty with an expensive hand wrapped in Rolex.

I let the bill hang and light a smoke.

"You folks taking a trip to Alcatraz?" I ask, pointing my cigarette above their heads to the mansion in the bay.

"Yes," says his orange skinned wife. I snatch the bill, and he grabs the painting. "This is our first time in California. We're trying to see everything."

"We must be going," he says.

"Well, take your needles and Bibles. It's a monastery now," I warn as this shitty couple wanders into the procession of loneliness with my last painting. I pick up my coffee can and flip a square of cardboard that reads *The Best Maine*

Woods Hippy Artist. I look in the direction of the Golden Gate Bridge and read aloud what the sign now says.

"Homeless and horny. All change will go to hookers and heroin."

7

Claire

The leaves have begun to turn, and the frost will surely follow. Toto plays tag with a dozen bewildered chickens, two of which are so young they've just witnessed their very first summer slip away. A pair of paper-dry leaves fall from the branch above and land on my lap, on the letter I'm writing to a Mr. Ryan Alexander, the boy on the tire swing from the photo Mom showed me. Thankfully, Grace was able to come up with his name after finishing a glass of champagne and another slice of pie.

I did an internet search and found out very little about him. He had a showing at a gallery in San Francisco last year. I called them, and the contact number they gave me is the number to China Wall Sushi. The lady that answered said she'd never heard of him. The gallery did give me an address, and so I have begun a letter, and hopefully he will get it; maybe he needs the money, and that land has got to be worth a lot, even if it is bought by, as Mom calls them, "scum".

Toto bounces over and sniffs the wet grass on my hands. A stray piece of clover sticks to the tip of his nose, but he doesn't seem to mind. I rub the white patch on his chest, and we watch an eagle soaring overhead. Toto warns the chickens with a bark, and they spot the predator. The lonely hollow erupts with the screams and clucks of frightened chickens. Some of the heavier layers waddle to safety while others tuck their wings, lean forward, and run like a band of tiny tanks.

Toto watches them scurrying until he's satisfied they're safe then looks back up with me, at the young eagle coasting on the currents coming off Apple Ridge: circling, watching, circling again, then turning to glide onward, down the mountain, over the mossy roof of Mr. Alexander's abandoned farmhouse, to follow the steep contours of Apple Ridge for the mile, or so, before the salty air above the Atlantic Ocean takes the baton and gives her brown and white mottled feathers lift.

Toto takes off, chasing a swarm of mayflies that hatched much too late from one of the ubiquitous creeks tumbling down this mountain. The sun, which no doubt tricked them into sprouting wings this morning, is warm on my bare legs, but the cold breeze rolling down Apple Ridge, which must be playing terror on these

22

fragile insects, makes me wish I'd put on more than shorts. I take the leaves off the letter, set them between my thighs and begin to write as Toto curls up next to me, yawns, then falls asleep.

As I write, I pause to take in the house below. It's silent down there, peaceful even. Brown vines run along the clapboards, encircling the windows below or reaching for the gutters above. To the right, the branches of a lone maple bow to the breeze, creating a kaleidoscope of golden light and gray shadows on the roof, and it becomes difficult for me to imagine that house is the same one where I met a five-year-old Ryan Alexander.

Ryan

"I need a bag, only one, though. I quit this morning," I say and empty a coffee can half-filled with dollar bills and change onto the kitchen table. "You have no idea how sore my throat is from earning this."

"How much is there?"

"Enough. Forty, maybe fifty."

"I'm not taking the time to count it. Benny, get over here."

"Here's a twenty," I say as I take the rich man's bill from my pocket.

A fourteen-year-old walks in looking like he wants to shank me.

"It'll cost you, white devil. I want a line."

"Step aside. I'll count it, then," I tell him.

"You should have counted before you came."

"Give him a line, or get out."

"Alright Benny," I say and rub his shaved head like he's a little bitch.

He goes for something under his button down, then he's held back.

"Just count the money. I don't want any blood anywhere near here.

"Amen to that," I say and open the curtain with a finger to watch a little boy and a pig-tailed girl pedaling by.

"Close that shit, man. We don't need anybody riding up on us."

I let the black curtain fall as Benny speaks.

"He's two dollars short."

"I knew I shouldn't have taken the blow job. Damn it all to hell, Benny! I should have taken the twenty-two eighty-two," I complain. "I'm giving your boy here a line. Cut me some slack?"

"Fine."

I open the baggie and drop a dime-sized pile of white on the table.

"Fuck's that?" he asks. "Drop some more."

"Eat that little man, and if you don't o.d., rip the next guy off, too," I say, and I'm out the door before Benny reaches for whatever's tucked under his shirt.

As I stroll through the park, the palms sway like Slender Man, and I think to leave, but some tourists are fake gang banging to Funky Cold Medina, and I kinda like that song. I sit on a bench on a hill that looks out over the city. Next to me is a toothless bum in white high tops. I get comfortable, cook the heroin and give myself one last shot before I get this monkey off my back for good this time. I hang around long enough for the shit to hit and burn half a cigarette.

"You should meet the crew back at my old place."

"It's going to rain any minute. Maybe you should get the fuck out of here, yourself," says the hobo.

"Probably for the best, my friend."

I stand up, creep with half-shut eyes to a tarred path and finish the cigarette on the walk to the palm trees.

An hour later and I'm at Nicole's. She isn't here, but the Volvo is. The front door's locked, so I climb in through a garage window I never shut. Inside are the few possessions I have. It's art stuff, mostly, and the shotgun that killed Dad. Maybe I'll pawn it all and buy another bag, maybe screw with Benny again.

I don't hear the car pulling in. I don't know anybody's home until the front door bangs shut. Nicole's heels tap the kitchen floor as she hums some emo song she was probably just listening to. A purse hits the granite island, high heels land on the designer couch and tumble to the floor. I'd listened to this every day for the year she let me live here after art school. Hearing it after not hearing it for a while is kind of nice.

She hates seeing me high, so I pull my sweatshirt's hood up and walk out the garage's back door. The clouds are black. The wind is strong, but the Pacific Ocean is calm. I light a Camel, sit down on a blue and white lawn chair, close my eyes, and ride the last few waves of opiate-bliss before it's washed out with the tide.

Not more than five minutes later, she wakes me up.

"You burnt my fucking lawn chair with that cigarette," she says as she jumps on me and kisses my neck. We both fall out of the chair and onto the crushed rock.

I rub my eyes and sit up.

"Sorry about the chair."

"It was ugly anyway. Do I need to ask why you're here? Are you finally going to take my hand in marriage? Or at least my underwear off?"

I shake my head.

"Where's your backpack?" she asks, knowing I travel light.

"In the garage."

"Alright, the cot's in the same place. I'll make some coffee," she says. "Come in. It's supposed to start raining."

Nicole goes toward the back door of the house, and as I stand there, rain begins to tap on my shoulder.

"You've got a huge stack of mail here. Ever think about getting a permanent address?"

"I have one," I say, walking toward her.

"Here?"

"Yep. Got any weed?"

"I just picked up an ounce."

"Heaven," I say, "I'm going to need it."

"Are you hooked again?"

"Yep."

"I'll roll a blunt," she says and steps inside, then pokes her head out. "Ryan."

"Yeah?"

"I've missed you a lot."

9

Ryan

"Sure you don't want to come inside? It'll be warmer in my bed," she says.

"No, that's okay."

"Your loss."

"I know it is."

"One of these days, Ryan Alexander, I'm going to get you," she says, flicks the light switch and closes the garage door, taking the little light coming in from the hallway with her.

I've got a cot, a pillow, a blanket, and a high from that blunt so strong it would knock out a crackhead, but I can't sleep, can't stop moving. Just because I'm not shaking doesn't mean the tremors aren't out to get me, you know?

After ordering Sushi from China Wall, Nicole helped me dig out my old art stuff from the boxes. We set it up, and I think I'll paint a little bit, just to see if I still can. I get out of the cot, reach around in the dark for the light switch. I find it, and the dim light glows grayish-yellow, making the garage look like a serial killer's basement.

I snag a one-inch filbert, laugh, and dip it in burnt sienna. I start with the nipples. She was big, fat and old, the owner of these nips,

28

and happened to be in front of me at Dink's Ice Cream in Bar Harbor, Maine when I was five. For whatever reason, I can't stop thinking about her. When she bent down to rub my head and tell me how cute I was, I could see down her shirt, and it was like popping a zit and wanting to see the puss splattered on the mirror. It was disgusting, my first realization that sharing skin and fluids is not for me.

Lightning strikes.

The palette slips from my hand and lands on the concrete. I peel the palette from the floor and dip the bristles in the smeared paint, which is mostly brown with marbled wisps of blue and red that explode from the center like the arms of a hurricane.

I consider what a hobo might say about having only what I have, and paint this memory of my childhood with a shit-brown background. When I finish with the last stroke, I kick my socks off, ruffle my hair, sit on the cot, finish a cigarette and then conk out with the light still on.

I wake up to a rocket fucking car horn.

"Ryan. Where are you?" Nicole hollers from outside the house. I don't say anything, but try to focus on just where the hell I am. I get up, turn the easel at an angle so when she comes in she can't see the half-porno.

"Where are you?" she hollers from outside.

"In the garage."

"Where, sexy?"

"The garage."

"Huh?" she asks, laughing, but the sound is deadened by the closed garage door.

"In your Mom's garage."

"Damn, Ryan. Low blow."

"You'd like to give me a low blow."

"I would, but you never let me."

"Life's fucked up as an asexual," I say while yawning.

"What was that? I don't think the neighbors heard you."

"Life's fucked up…"

"It only makes me want you more," she says.

"It's not because of my looks," I say while placing my fingertips on the garage door.

"Whatever. You know how I know you're gay?" she asks.

"How?"

I knock on the metal between us.

"Because you're too good looking to be straight," she says, knocking back.

"I ain't gay, either."

"I'll be right in."

The house's front door squeaks. Heels tap, fingers drum, emo hum, clutch slap, two shoes topple.

"I just went shopping. I bought a ton of munchies," she says as she opens the door connecting the house to the garage and throws me an orange soda. "I got all your favorites."

"What happened to work?" I ask.

"It was an outside scene. They wanted sunshine, and the universe wanted rain. No movie

30

making today." She smiles, blinks, puts her hands on her hips.

"What film are you working on now?"

"Romcom."

"Sounds lame as fuck."

"It is," she says. "I'm leaving for Massachusetts in a couple of days to film a college scene."

"There aren't any colleges in California?"

"Sure, but they're not as pretty, and it takes place in the fall. We need the colors of New England foliage."

"Makes sense."

"Okay. Off you go, bring in the groceries for me. I'll get started on making lunch. John's throwing a party tonight. Remember him?"

"Dick."

"Well, he's got an open house at the art gallery for some new artists, like what he did for you. Maybe you could talk to him?"

"I don't paint anymore."

"What about that?" she asks while pointing at the easel.

"My hands are shaking too much. It was just a joke, anyway."

She pulls a joint out from her bra, lights it and passes it to me.

"Maybe this will slow down the shakes. I know you're having a hard time, but it doesn't seem as bad as before," she says.

"I wasn't using for very long, just enough to get hooked."

"Good," she says. "Then this should be easier. Can I see the what's on the easel?"

I step aside.

"Are those nipples?"

"Pretty nice, though, huh?"

"Love it."

"Cool," I say.

"Let's go inside. I'm starving."

I follow her into the kitchen, and she points to a stack of mail overflowing a shoebox.

"Will you go through that?"

"Throw it away," I say.

"Screw you. You throw it away. I put in all the effort to save it for you, and you just want me to toss it?"

I shrug.

"I don't need anything," I explain.

I grab the pile and drop it in the trash.

"Now it's full, and you've got to take it out," she says.

"Gawd," I complain and bring it out to the street.

"They don't pick up the trash for three more days," she tells me when I come back in.

"You know how punctual I am. So, what're you making to eat?" I ask.

"Chips from a bag. Ho-ho's, maybe."

"I love Ho-Ho's."

"I know. Here, this came for you today. Put it in the garbage if you want, but I refuse to. It's a felony if I do that."

She throws it at me like a ninja star. I walk ten feet behind me and pick it up off the floor.

"It's from back home," I say. "Ruby Lane…"

"That has to be worth opening," Nicole says. "Give it to me."

"Fine, but like a decent, caring individual, I choose to deliver, rather than turn it into a weapon."

I pass her the letter.

"Well, the person that wrote this has beautiful handwriting, and, oh, you're rich," she says.

"Loaded."

"Here, take it. Some farm wants to buy your family's land."

"We still own that? Nobody's paid taxes on that place in a decade," I say as a grab the letter.

"I guess the town hasn't claimed it yet. Your parents must have paid it off."

"Jesus, I haven't been near a farm in a long time. How am I supposed to get back?"

"You can have the Volvo."

"I can't take your car. Just lend me a hundred bucks for a bus ticket, and once I reach the end of the Golden Road, I'll send you back everything I owe."

"Keep it, Ryan. You should have your own things."

"American bums don't need stuff."

"What's an American bum?"

"Kind of like me, but a bit more American bummish."

"Think of it this way. The car can be mine, not yours, that you're only using. I don't drive it anymore, anyway. I don't know if you noticed the Lexus out front, or not."

"I haven't left the garage. I figured you were still driving the Volvo."

"Here," she opens a counter drawer, pulls out a set of keys with a Kool cigarette keychain I found in a gutter five years ago.

"I still remember when we drove it across the country after college," I say while looking down at the name on the envelope.

"Why are you smiling?" she asks.

"I just remembered I know the girl who wrote this. She got me into art school," I say and tuck the letter into my pants pocket.

"How?"

"I just met her one summer when we were kids, and I painted us on this old tire swing on my lawn. It was the only thing I brought in my admissions portfolio," I say as nausea pools in my stomach.

"Is that the one you hung in our apartment in college?"

"It is."

I sit down in a kitchen chair.

"Are you feeling okay? You look like ass."

"I'm going to puke," I say. "Detox sucks."

"Come on," she says, hooking an arm through mine. "Bathroom. Now."

34

10
Ryan

"Hey, Babe. I'm back. Hope you're feeling better. I just got China Wall," she says.

"What about John's party tonight?" I ask while walking into the kitchen with my duffel bag in one hand and my father's shotgun in the other.

"I only brought him up to make you jealous."

"I love your honesty."

"Got the gun out, huh?" she asks.

"Yeah. I should bring it with me. It's probably better home, anyway. Can't be letting it get into Benny's hands."

"Who's Benny?"

"Just some smart-talking bitch."

"Dealer?"

"Something like that. The rain's stopped," I say, pointing through the open door to the glossy stone walkway.

"I know. Finally, right? I'm sorry I'm late."

She leans against the counter and clasps her hands above her heart.

"Stay one more night. Will you? I want to see you as long as I can," she says.

"All goodbyes are murderous goodbyes. Let's just do it here."

"You never had a problem leaving before."

"Sure I did. That's why I didn't tell you."

"Did it work, though?"

"No," I lie.

"So, maybe you're wrong?"

"Fine. Okay. Maybe."

She puts her hands on her hips and searches the kitchen.

"Okay, I think you're all set. There's a credit card in the glove box for gas, food, whatever. Here's my cell. I still have my work phone if you need me."

"I don't even know how to use these things," I say as I grab the phone. "Any good music?"

"The Supremes to Manson and everything in between."

"Kesha?"

"Of course."

"Cool."

"Just hit this button. I'm speed dial one."

"I'll pay you back times ten when I sell the land," I say.

"Don't worry about it. Your art stuff is packed. Also, I found two old paintings of yours."

"I thought I had sent them all out."

"So, you should be all set."

"Best mosey along then," I say. I throw the backpack on my shoulder, look around the kitchen one last time. Nicole jumps up, wrapping her arms and legs around me. "I'll call once I get there."

"Are you going to eat?" she asks, setting her feet on the floor and opening the styrofoam boxes. "Here, take this and this. Napkins are in the bag."

"You're too good to me," I say. "You treat me like a prince when I'm really a pecker."

She puts her hands on my shoulders, turns me around, and kicks me in the ass.

"Get out of here you asexual weirdo before I rape you."

"I'm going. I'm going."

"Ryan," she asks, and I look back over my shoulder while walking to the car. "Can you ever love me?"

"I don't know, Nicki. I've got to go.

11
Claire
Mom and I are at the kitchen table, playing cribbage like Mary and Grace from the

Grange probably are. Maybe Grace is already dead and Mary's waiting her turn out of politeness. I found an old picture frame Gram wasn't using and put the photo of Ryan and me riding the tire swing in it and placed it on the kitchen table, just in front of the window sill.

"A happier time," I explain to Mom.

In the center of the frosted window pane to my right, behind the picture frame, is an opening the size of a book cover where I scraped the frost away. Through this miniature doorway in the window, we neglect the cards in our hands for the moment and watch the snowflakes sift down outside the window pane. Some catch on the sill and begin to pile up, looking like mountains trapped in a snow globe.

"It usually only snows this early in Canada," Mom says as she sips her coffee.

"This happens every year. It'll be gone before you know it," I say.

Mom turns around and reaches into her coat that's draped over her chair, pulls a joint out from the breast pocket, and lights it.

"No more vaporizer?" I ask.

"Sometimes you just need to light up. Sure you don't want to try it? Fifteen-two," she says while laying down a queen of hearts on a five of spades and then passes me the joint. "It's supposed to help with cancer."

"What am I supposed to do with it? I mean, how?"

"You never smoked a cigarette?"

38

"Once, in tenth grade, when Becky was over."

"She was always a little whore."

"She was only sixteen."

"I miss cigarettes more than sex. Just inhale and hold it in, like you're sipping coffee through a straw."

"Sorry, Mom," I say, as I lay down a queen on her queen. I move my peg forward two holes, take my first sip of pot and pass it back. "I don't feel any different."

"Just wait," she says as she taps the ash into her empty coffee cup. "So, do you miss work, yet? Is that why you're teaching that poetry class at the Grange?"

"It's on the Psalms. It's not my kind of poetry. Anyway, I've been hung up on this Ryan guy."

"Why?"

"Don't know. Maybe I'm bored?"

"Isn't that why you're delving into the Good Book with all those old people?"

"Maybe."

"Maybe you have a crush on an imaginary boy," she says.

"Maybe I'm going to answer that," I say as I get out of the chair and pick up the phone.

"Hello?"

"Hey, Claire, it's me."

"Who?"

"Your sexy penpal from a distant land, Nuk-Nuk."

"Ryan?" I ask.

"Maybe," he says deeply, seductively.

I sit back down at the kitchen table and cover the receiver.

"It's him, I think," I whisper to Mom.

"Who?"

"Him. He's absolutely crazy."

"How did you know it was me?" he asks.

"What? How did you hear that?"

"Fucking bionic," he explains.

"How did he hear you," asks Mom.

"He's a robot."

"I just left my alleyway in San Francisco. I'm letting you know I'm on my way."

"Great," I say. "Mom found some pictures of us from when we were kids."

"I want to see them. I kind of remember you."

"I think so, too."

"I hope this isn't weird, me calling and all. I'm heading into the Mojave, haven't seen anyone in hours and felt like talking to an old friend."

"It's not weird. Calling it weird makes it weird. You might be a little weird."

"He seems a little weird," says Mom.

"Who do you keep talking to?"

"My mother. How did you get my number? I must be easier to find than you are."

"Four-one-one. Thanks for the letter. I'm keeping it forever. Sorry to hear about ole' Cass. I always liked her," he says.

"Gram had a long life."

Mom sifts through the music on my mp3 player, picks a Lana Del Rey album, and we hear how she tastes like Pepsi Cola. I walk to the living room, part the curtains and notice the early sun trying to burn through a snowy overcast.

"Hello?" he says.

"Hello."

"Something wrong?"

"No. I'm just trying to picture what you look like now from your voice," I say. "I wonder how you've changed."

"What's my voice say?"

"I'm still trying to figure it out."

"Are you blushing?" he asks.

"Why would you think that?"

"I just remember that one summer when we were kids, you used to blush a lot, especially when we rode the tire swing."

"I thought you barely remembered me?" I question.

"Maybe I do. Maybe I don't. So, are you blushing or not?"

"Maybe I am. So what?"

"Just means you're still cute," he says and hangs up.

I sit down with Mom at the kitchen table, pick up my cards, and fan the marijuana smoke away from my face.

"Crazy?" asks Mom.

"In a good way," I tell her.

"You still have a crush on him, don't you?"

"Cut it out. I think I'm starting to feel the pot."

"Sounds like you're dope crazy," she says, and as we sit, I watch how the hovering smoke spirals and swishes between us with each pulse of laughter. "Do you want some hot chocolate?"

"I'd love some," she says.

"Oh. He's coming in a couple of days. We should get the heat and electricity turned on for him."

"My darling Claire," she says, "you do that for him, and I'll get the marshmallows for us."

"And when we're done, we meet in front of the television and watch Gilmore Girls."

"Deal," she says.

12
Ryan

California's gone, and it's night. I am erased. If it wasn't for the two paintings Nicole found, the twelve-gauge and a few boxes of art supplies, I'd have no idea who I am, somewhere between clean and high, straight and bent, dead and alive.

There's no traffic out here. No bums. No junk. Completely dead. Black. Austere. Barren. Desolate. My Dad's loaded shotgun's been riding shotgun all trip. I pick it up, rest the stock on my lap and the barrel to the door.

There hasn't been a car since the sun went down, and the only thing more boring than sobriety is the awareness of it. I talked to Claire today, found her number real sly and shit and dialed it with the phone Nicole gave me.

The low gas light blinks.

Twenty miles of blackness later and there's a gas station lit by a single flickering lamp. There are pumps so old they don't take credit cards, and I don't care, 'cause I ain't got cash.

I unscrew the gas cap, plug her in, squeeze the handle and gasoline starts flowing without having to speak a word to a cashier. God blesses those who distrust.

Someone turns in, shooting high beams, and pulls in behind me, cranking Poison, or Bon Jovi, or maybe it's Eighteen Visions. They honk, laugh like demons, and their SUV starts shaking.

"Is that Winger?"

"Where's the rock at, hippy?" screams a guy out of the passenger's window.

"No idea. Not from here. Don't touch that stuff," I holler over the ripping guitar solo.

"You won't find much dick out here, fag," says the driver after turning down the Winger.

"I've already found two, and this is my first stop."

I hang up the gas nozzle, jump in the Volvo and take off. Their exhaust screams as they peel out, and their headlights remain high.

"Might as well take care of this now," I say and put the shotgun back on my lap, the barrel to the door. The trigger is familiar, like smelling home after years away and for a second, I don't miss heroin so much. I lead them a few miles away from the gas station, further into the desert, take my foot off the pedal and coast annoyingly slow. They pull next to me. Show me the old finger. Call me a homo. One of them licks his nipple.

My car creeps so slow, slower, then slow again. The guy in the passenger's seat gets out and walks along side my rolling car. I light a Camel and hang an elbow out the window. Seeing his white face in the headlights blowing up this black night is really something, like watching Brad Pitt on the big screen.

"You ain't got no meth, how about a cigarette?" he asks.

The Volvo finally stops. I don't get out, but rub the shotgun's trigger with the pad of my finger.

He puts his elbows on the roof and looks out as far as the yellow headlights and red taillights press into the night.

"Did Momma teach you how to mix batteries and cold pills, Billy-Bob?" I ask while lifting the barrel.

He unzips his pants and pisses down the side of the Volvo.

"You said you wanted it," he says.

"I cannot argue, for I am a peaceful bean."

The driver honks, laughs, then stands on the gas and the brakes; the truck roars and black smoke hides the headlights.

I click off the safety.

"You've probably got a hard-on, don't you?" he asks as the air clears.

The trigger's pulled. The black night is white. The whole world burns and for a second there's nothing, nothing at all, then their exhaust explodes, and the desert vanishes as the exhaust gets quieter and quieter until it's only me, half a man, a black desert, and the gray air hanging above us all. I start the Volvo and go on gentle into this good night.

13
Claire

When the doctor first told me I had cancer, we came here, Mom, Toto and I. We laid down on this rock I'm now on. It juts into River Pond like a panhandle. The waves roll now, as they did that night, over the smooth tip, and it sounds like a distant, lapping ocean.

We didn't move all night, not as the sky turned from blue to red to pink to a silvery blue-gray, then to black. We stayed on this rounded rock. We didn't leave when the fire burnt out. We didn't leave when the loon sounded like a frightened ghost, and we all got scared. We didn't leave until after the black sky became a drab blue-gray, then pink, then red, and blue again.

It was true mourning: the second day. Amen.

14
Ryan
Ten Years Ago

I take the shotgun, wipe the trigger and toss it next to him on my bed.

"Is there any pain in dying? Anything at all?"

He jerks his head to the left and shows me his rotten fettuccine-brain.

"How could you do that to Mom? You never should have done that."

His eyelids bow then raise, his eyes molested by the pain.

"The world was never meant for someone as beautiful as you, Vincent," is all that he says as his eyes close.

"But you're a Dali man."

15
Ten years and a day or two later

Ryan

This is the first I've seen fall leaves
since I left for California with Nicole when I
was twenty, a day after dropping out of art
school. This is upstate New York, and only a few
leaves have turned here, so that means Maine's
foliage is on fire. The morning's easy on the
eyes and the mind. The withdrawals, which weren't
shit this time, are just about the fuck outta
here. The sun's out, frost sheets the windows,
and the whole world is way too bright for tired
eyes.
    I yawn, stretch, yawn again, light a smoke,
grab a coke, the half-eaten bag of peanuts, and
hop out of the Volvo where I slept between two
boxes of shit I don't need. There's the cold.
It's frozen, pleasurable in a sadistic way, a VHS
of childhood memories. I pull the hood over my

head and check out the field I parked in last night; Nobody's looking for me way out here. The desert's a few cultures back, you know?

It goes a long way away, this field, and I don't know these mountains or that stream, but I feel like I do. They're like all the goddamn mountains around my home, the stream, the smell, but I'm in New York and not Maine.

I hit the cig, go to get in the driver's seat and see a fleck of brown blood on the blue door. I pick at it with my thumbnail, only because it seems like the right thing to do, then get in the driver's seat, take a sip of coke, start the car.

"Dick," I say to the check engine light.

I flick the cigarette out the window and light another, then close my eyes, press the gas, listen to the unnatural metallic drum roll coming from under the hood and move on down from upstate, not stopping until reaching the Casco Bay Bridge in Maine where I slide the shotgun into the departing tide and take a nap.

16
Claire

One day, my perfume is blown across the woodland. The next, only the smell of damp grass and dying leaves mutters around; I am Dylan Thomas's flower.

Toto and I are outside on the porch, looking down the lawn at the neglected farmhouse cowering at the edge of the field. He jumps down, leaps off the five steps to the rock path leading to the driveway. A healthy gray squirrel climbs a tree while chattering down at him. Toto barks back, turns around, hops up on the porch and onto my lap.

I pull the wool hat over my ears as the early fall chill settles in, and I become dizzy while watching a couple of chickens dig and bathe in the driveway dirt. A heavy-whirling-swishing wave crashes into me, filling my stomach with wiggling maggots. I try to stand. Toto leaps down.

"Mom! Mom! Help," I scream, or do I? I don't know. My head is a brick. My knees fail. I fall. The front door swings open.

"Are you okay, Claire?"

She crouches, rubs my back, then, when the dizziness fades, helps me upstairs.

Mom takes me to the bathroom so I can be sick in a sickly place. I finish, rinse my face with the coldest water from the bottom of the well, then brush my teeth. Mom takes the trash bag and, before leaving, runs a bath for me.

I come down an hour later with a steady stomach and sneak into the kitchen to watch Mom as she washes the dishes and sings to herself. A tear falls down my cheek, and I think she hears it hit the floor because she turns around, hurries over and wraps two soapy arms around me.

"Why were you sick? Are you taking your medications?" she asks.

"No."

"Why not?"

I sit at the kitchen table and look at the photo of Ryan and me as children.

"Mom, please don't forget I watched Gram die from chemo while you were home. I'm going on my terms."

"Honey. Please."

"I had a test done on my liver the day I left the university. They took some samples from the cancer. They might be able to take out part of my liver, and I'll be fine. I didn't want to tell you because it's less than a ten percent chance."

She throws her arms around me and soaks the collar of my shirt with tears. Then, when she catches her breath, sits opposite me and holds my hands across the table, gazing with a stupefied hope in her eyes that has more than a ninety percent chance of causing her more devastation than she's ever known.

17
Ryan

The goddamned car's dead. It died this morning when I went for a walk around my old art school in Portland, Maine. I tinkered around under the hood: lifted hoses, wiggled wires, kicked tires. Who knows this stuff? Not me. I called a salvage yard. They towed it and gave me four hundred bucks. Now I'm on the sidewalk outside the apartment Nicole and I shared in college with my shit, trying to blend in with itchy meth heads and a group of Somali refugees warming their hands around a trash can fire.

I lean against a blue mail drop off and pretend I'm some sexy greaser as I light this Camel.

The phone Nicole gave me rings.

"Ryan. Where are you?"

"Hey, Nicki. I'm outside our old apartment. The Volvo broke down. I thought you said it never breaks down?"

"Hi. It never has. Shepley! You're at MECA?"

"Yeah. What's up?" I ask.

"Nothing. I just thought you'd be at your house by now. I wanted to make sure you made it."

"Haven't left Portland. I stopped by to check it out, took a walk around Congress, and then the car died. I'm hiking to the bus station

52

in a few minutes. I just need to figure out what
to do with all my stuff on the sidewalk."

"Oh. Be safe. I love you," she says.

"Thanks."

"I was also calling to ask if you had any
time to think about what I said?"

"You said?"

"About us. About you ever loving me?"

"Oh, yeah," I say. "You were serious?"

"I guess I'll talk to you later then."

She hangs up.

There is no sun and no moon, just brick and
concrete and dirty asshole bums. I step off a
crunchy sheet of ice spanning the storm drain and
up onto the curb. Some art kid ventured out here
from the nicer part of the city and sits cross-
legged on the street corner painting the other
street corner. I walk down to the Cigarette
Shopper, buy two packs and walk back to my stuff
to find a toothless guy and his Olive Oil chick
going through my shit.

"Just leave the backpack, dickheads."

"Can I borrow your lighter?" asks a black
haired girl in tight red pants.

I pass her a lighter.

"Are those for sale?" she asks, pointing to
the two paintings the bums hadn't thought about
taking.

"They're not worth anything. I'll trade
them for a bag," I say.

"I don't sell pot," she says.

"Pot? That's cute."

"What I do sell is a good time, though,"
she says, rubbing her shoulder on me.
"Yeah? You got balloons and waterslides?"
"In a womanly sort of way, yes."
"Watch out for the ice," I say, nodding
toward the storm drain.
"I'll give you half-off. Fifty for the
whole show," she says.
"You're probably the hottest, cleanest
hooker I've ever seen. You should be the manager
at a goth savings bank or something."
"Whatever. Aren't you going to stop them
from stealing your stuff?"
I turn around, suck in a drag, then flick
the cigarette into the street.
"It's nothing. Here," I say and give her
most of the cash the salvage guy gave me for the
Volvo. "Take this cassette, too."
"What's this for?"
"Don't do this shit anymore. Bums don't
fuck for money," I say.
"Everyone sells their body to someone."
"Maybe you should be a communist instead."
"What's wrong with you, man?"
"I know you don't understand, but Jesus
loves you anyway," I say and study her mouth as
she chews on a lip ring. "True story."
"What about the tape? Is this nineteen
ninety-four."
"The Jesus Lizard will save your life,
too."
We go over to the tweaker Olive Oil walking
away with an armload of blank canvases, leaving

my two paintings behind to be studied by refugees
who don't take, but only look. They smile and
pull their winter coats tighter as I kneel beside
the paintings, flick the lighter and set them on
fire.

"Warm your hands, boys," I say.

"It looks like somebody lit a shot of 151,"
says the hooker.

"I need to get to the Greyhound."

"Stranded?"

"Yeah," I say, bending to warm my hands
over the fire with the others.

"Cars are for suits, anyway," she says.

"Not everyone can ride in your back seat,"
I explain then stand, look into the dull blue
eyes of an intelligent stranger, give her a
smooch on her swollen lips, pick up my duffel
bag, then head toward the airport to find a bus.

18
Ryan
The inside smells like every bus station, ever,
just like greasy hair and gasoline. Airplanes
keep flying by and playing black metal riffs with
their engines; It's so fucking irritating.

"Anyone hear?" I ask.

A head pokes out from behind the office
door.

"What can I do you for?"

"A Coke and a Moon Pie usually works," I
say.

"What?"

"Nothing. My car died over on Shepley."

"Okay," she says.

"It just stopped running. Only Click-click. No vroom-vroom," I say and put all my money on the counter. "I need a ticket to Bangor and a bag of heroin."

"So sorry," she says as she slops wet chewing gum. "That'll be leaving in an hour. Here's your ticket and the change."

"Eighty-two cents, I presume?"

"Correct. I hope you're day brightens."

"Thanks. You too. I'll just be over here by the piss can."

It's warmed up in this cold city, so I spend the hour smoking cigarettes and smelling burgers and fries from the Applebee's across the road. An old man walks up as an airplane thunders by. Once the world shakes the headache, I ask him where he thinks the plane's going.

"Bottom of the fucking ocean, for all I care. This is the most I've talked in twenty-two years."

He takes a homeless chug from a small paper bag and keeps on walking, not paying any attention to the floppy sole on his boat shoe.

19

Claire

It's odd to think about suicide in Church;
it's like taking a nap in a casket. I'm not in a
service, but down in the basement of the Grange
Hall where they sometimes hold prayer meetings.
I've just finished teaching about the prosody of
the Psalms to a group of elderly women who are
currently hobbling up the stairs. So, for
tonight, it is a Church, as well as a hospice.

I should want nothing more than to go home
and check my messages. The doctor's office is
supposed to call to give me news about fixing me
for good. I've been willfully forgetting about it
since my last day at work when I had the initial
appointment, and now the time's here, and I don't
want to know, don't want to hear the gavel fall.

I take the coffee pot over to the double
basin sink: empty, rinse, dry, then set it back
in the cupboard next to the paper plates still in
their plastic sheath. I put the Bibles back into
the closet, turn the lights off, and, unable to
think of anything else to do, go upstairs.

Once Mom and I are outside, I thank the
cold air for cooling me off. The stars are out,
and Andromeda spins as my mother puts her arms
around me.

"Warm enough for you?" she asks.

"Mom," I say, leaning my head on her shoulder. Her winter coat is like a pillow on my cheek. "Mom, I'm nervous."

"We'll listen together, honey."

20
Claire

The red light from the answering machine blinks in a black room. One pulse. One message. Mom grabs my hand; I flip on the kitchen light, and she presses play.

Hello, Claire. This is Janet Walker from Doctor Baley's office. I'm calling to let you know that your tumor is too large for a partial hepatectomy. If you have any questions, please call the office anytime between eight and five, Monday through Friday, to speak with a staff nurse.

The burden becomes too heavy for my legs, and I collapse. Mom comes with me.

"Will you please reconsider medication and chemo?" she pleads while holding me. "Please, honey?"

"No! I saw what it did to Gram. I watched her die. It won't be me. Never."

I grab my stomach and choke on the quick pain.

"What's the matter? Claire? Claire?!"

Mom squeezes my shoulder, and the world darkens. A phone's being dialed.

"I need an ambulance to Ruby Lane. Now."

21
Ryan

A couple of hours shy of a day later, and I'm getting off a Greyhound on Main Street in Bangor. I hurry to cross the bridge into Brewer, just so I can get that shithole out of the way, and four hundred and forty feet before of a half-mile, eight feet from a guy stalking munchkins behind a Dunkin Donuts, a couple picks me up in a dope Cadillac. They don't talk much, which doesn't bother me because they're Canadian.

First thing I notice when we get into Cherryfield is all the eighteen-wheelers with "Ocean Side" written on the doors. I've counted five, so far, carrying snorting, seeing pigs who will soon hang from chains and experience their skin boiling away.

59

"Thanksgiving," says the driver in his shitty French-English.

"Yeah. Kill them fuckers," I say, and the car goes quiet until just before Ruby Lane when I begin to see the procession of aluminum buildings disguised as barns.

"My stop's right up here."

"Okay," says the driver as he pulls over and I get out.

"Aur Revoir. Je t'aime," I say.

"Good. Good. Bye-bye. Love you too. Hehe."

Fucking Canadians.

I toss the backpack over my shoulder and check out the nasty factory farm across Route 1 that wasn't there when I left. I turn around, look up the shaded dirt road called Ruby Lane where, a mile in, is my house, and take a step forward, beginning the long journey up the mountain.

A ways in, I wipe the sweat from my forehead, step into the shade, take out the letter Claire wrote me and fan my face with it. Ruby Lane's grown in. It used to be thin, fragile. It could have been mistaken for an abandoned logging road. Now it's like a railroad tunnel, beautiful, but dark, clean, barely wide enough for a vehicle.

Up ahead is a bright square the size of a school buses ass. Through that hole is the secluded world where I grew up. Few things rattle me. I've never felt much, but this makes me feel.

22
Claire

"You think he'll be here today? Is that why you're sitting out here?"

"No, Mom. I'm sitting out here because it's a beautiful afternoon, and I'm finally rested after leaving the hospital."

"Do you want some more iced tea?"

"No, thanks. This one's still full."

"Mind if I sit down?"

"Of course not."

"What're you reading?"

"The Bell Jar. My beautiful students got it for me as a going away gift."

"I remember when I first bought that for you. You couldn't put it down."

"A week after you bought it I made you take me to Smith to find her old dorm."

"It was a fun summer vacation. Wasn't it?"

"Very much. It's one of my favorite memories shared with my darling mother. I had a lot of fun at Storyland, too."

"Remember the roller coaster? You were so scared."

"Of course. It was the best. That was also the summer I met Ryan."

We stop and look out over the field.

"It was a busy one. I want to thank you for taking some medication," she says.

"Marijuana and opiates… how a straightedge girl handles cancer."

"You haven't even taken any yet."

"Maybe someday."

Toto rockets off the porch and barks.

"Mom, I think that's him."

"Where?"

"Coming up the road, down by his driveway."

"I think I see."

"He's taller than I remember."

"How can you tell from so far away?"

"Because he was four feet tall last time I saw him."

"About as tall as you, Claire?"

"Close."

"Let's go introduce ourselves," she says.

"Not yet."

"I hear you," Ryan calls as he disappears into the shade of his house and, a moment later, hollers "fucking bionic hearing!"

"I guess the sound travels well here," I say.

"I guess so."

23
Ryan

There's home: a two-story farmhouse hiding in the shade of two mammoth red maples. Here's the dry-rotted tire underneath the tree where I met Claire. It used to hang from a rope but that frayed, dried and blew away a long time ago. Now just a fragment, a loose, tattered knot, circles the branch like a wedding ring. I walk over and pick out the wet leaves from inside the tire then look over the house's roof to the still weathervane perched on the barn's peak. I never cry, but I do today.

The rotting deck is spongy under my feet. It, like everything, returns home. I open the door, my heart beating in my wrist, and walk in with closed eyes, trying to think about pleasant things like heroin, tire swings, and an empty home, but as my eyelids open, I find the room blurry from tears. I leave my footprints in the dust while walking to the couch. It's hard to believe I used to watch Looney Tunes on this. I flip the couch cushions, sneeze thrice, sit in front of an empty fireplace and wait to die again.

When I was a kid, we went to Disneyland. There was this haunted house that I've never been able to forget. I used to paint it a lot. Aside from my family not being here, this house reminds me of that. I go to the rolltop desk and pretend it's the same grand piano the ghost played during that ride while he was in his study, and we were in his dark.

I should be moving on up the hill to introduce myself to the belle, but I need to lie down; I need a shower. I would've gone all the way up there first if I wasn't so out of shape and dirty. Slumming and hitching around San Francisco is a lot easier than hiking Ruby Lane. I get up, flick the switch by the door and the lights come on without me having to make one call to the electric company.

24
Claire

I don't remember the walk down Ruby Lane taking this long. Maybe because it's dark. Maybe because Apple Ridge has heated up after an early October chill, and I want to linger in the secrecy of new air in a warm night. I adjust Ryan's mailbox so it stands a little straighter

64

then walk toward the front door. I tried to clean his yard before he came, and as I melt into my first painkiller high, its organic beauty surprises me, like I'm walking through any New England postcard. I scuff my bare feet on the cold gravel and turn toward his house. Walking into the glow of the outside light, I go up the steps to knock on the door, but it opens before my knuckles tap.

"Nice hobo shoes," he says while raising a cigarette to his mouth.

"My feet?" I ask, looking down at the naked toes.

Ryan nods, and the left corner of his mouth curls into a smile as he speaks.

"Have we changed at all?"

"Maybe a little."

"Maybe," he agrees.

"Well, Ryan, it's nice to meet you again," I say, handing him the letter from Ocean Side.

"Is this my golden ticket?"

"If money's what you want, there it is." I look back at the tire on the lawn. "There's not much left of the swing."

"It's still there. We just need a rope," he explains.

"Then we shall get one."

A gust of night-wind blows dead leaves across the lawn; it takes a moment for the dry tumbling to stop before words interrupt autumn perfection.

"Were you coming to see me shirtless?" I ask.

"Sure. That sounds great," he says.

"Not me! You. Are you going to put a shirt on?"

"Oh," he says, "just a sec. Come in. Come in."

The living room's lit with bursts of orange and red from the fireplace. Ryan's knelt by a gym bag searching for a shirt, and I try to decipher some of the different tattoos on his arms, but I can only make out Sisyphus and his rock.

"This'll do," he says and pulls on a Kesha t-shirt.

"Seriously?"

"What? She's hella dope. I saw her with Rihanna."

"Hella," I affirm and sit on the couch.

"Did you get all this turned on? The gas, the lights, the water?" he asks.

"Yep. Right after you called."

"Thanks."

He goes over to a pile of books and photos and other things I can't quite tell and fills the fireplace with them.

"Guess I should have ordered some firewood," I say.

"Naw. This isn't for heat."

"If not heat, then what?"

"Ambiance," he says.

"I'm flattered. Have you eaten dinner?" I ask. "Mom's making french toast."

25
Ryan

"Ring-ring-ring," says the phone.

"Fuck-fuck-fuck," says my mouth.

I kick the covers off, stretch, tell the world it's crap for making heroin unsustainable for the hobo, go out on the balcony, gallop down the stairs, and answer the rotary relic screwed to the kitchen wall.

"Hey, baby. It's Nicole."

"What up?"

"Were you sleeping?"

"Was."

"It's three o'clock," she says.

"Yeah, there."

"Whatever. It's still noon in Maine, bum."

"True. I had to get up anyway. Claire and I are going to talk to the Ocean Side guys. What's happening?"

"Not much. I'm just getting ready to fly to Massachusetts. The shoot got delayed. How're you doing?"

"Fine. I just got in. Things are tight."

"Good. I want to make this quick."

"Like a band-aid?"

"Do you have an answer yet… to my question?"

I take a big, smokeless, sober breath.

"Eeeeeeeeeek," I say as I get in a killer
stretch from fingertip to toe tip. "Nicole, I
love you, I do, but you know I can't love anybody
like that. Ain't got it in me. Not even you, the
greatest woman in this world. I'm sorry. I'm
hopeless."

"You will change one day, Ryan, and I hope
I'm still here."

"Nicki, don't."

"Goodbye, Ryan."

She hangs up.

"eh-eh-eh-eh," says the phone.

I hang it up and start some coffee. Claire
had this whole place put together. I can't
believe it. She even brought down milk, cereal,
blue, brown, white and green eggs from her
chickens. They're beautiful art. I won't eat the
green and blue eggs, just the brown and white.

"Knock-knock," says the door.

God, I hope it's Mr.Junky Man. I hope it's
drugs. I hope little, underage Benny got in his
hoopty and scooted on over to Maine, but he'd
haul out two twenty-two's and knock on the door
with the strength of ten men, and this is the
tapping of a creature much smaller: a petite
fille.

"Coming, dear. Hey, my little letter
writer. Where's your car?" I ask, opening the
door and looking over the short girl in a red
bandana to an empty driveway.

"That's Toto," she says about the wiry mutt
circling my ankles.

"Nice to meet you. Car?"

68

"I thought we could walk. Ocean Side isn't too far."

We step outside, and I follow her and the mutt out of the driveway and down this mountain.

"Wait for me," someone hollers from behind.

"Mom, hurry up," says Claire.

"Mind if I tag along?" she asks.

"Mom, this is Ryan. Ryan, this is Mom."

"Pleased," I say, taking her hand and giving it a peck. Toto stands on his hind feet and drums my leg. "Hey, little guy," I say as we begin our stroll down Ruby Lane. "I'll keep going only if Claire carries me back up."

"Fine," she says.

"Fine? Fine? What do you mean 'fine'? You're like this big, and I'm like this big."

I light a cigarette. She looks up at me, squints, but not before the sun sets her eyes on fire.

"This isn't California. You need to toughen up," says her Mom.

"Mom's not complaining, and she's fresh out of Georgia," Claire says.

"Huff. Fine. Geez. You're carrying me if I need it."

We start to talk about Cass, then we move on to Claire, me, and the tire swing. Sylvia brings up amusement parks. In between the words, though, we listen to the sounds Claire's bare feet make as they fling bits of gravel down the cold, dirt road, sounding like the inside of a tipped hour glass.

26

Sylvia

Ryan, Claire and I cross the road and go into the parking lot outside Ocean Side. A half-dozen farm trucks sit idling without anyone in the driver's seat. As we walk together across the parking lot, Claire stays a half-step in front of us.

"How are your feet not cold?" he asks.

"Oh, how you don't know my daughter."

"How is your face not cold?" she asks.

"Should we get Toto?"

"He knows not to cross the road. We'll get him on the way back," says Claire.

"Monkish," he says, and walks toward the main office, lights another cigarette and pans the land, which consists of a pasture filled with windowless, silver barns.

"Let's go," he says, blowing out a lungful of smoke, and when the dry, acrid smell goes under my nose, I miss the days when I smoked cigarettes.

"These monkeys won't let us within fifty feet of an animal," I tell him.

"I don't know. Something interesting, I guess. I've got half a fresh butt and about five minutes to kill."

"Fresh butt?" I ask as Claire whistles.

"Mmmmmmm," he says.

"Let's at least try," says Claire.

Just as we step out of the parking lot and go toward the barns, an overweight employee in a red t-shirt stops us.

"Told you," I say.

"Can we help you?"

"Just looking around, Chap," Ryan says.

"For what?" he asks.

"Some drugs. You got any drugs, maybe a kilo of the finest white?"

"Can you please stay in the parking lot. Farm policy is to not let people roam, on account of insurance, and all."

"Oh, yes, insurance," says Ryan. "Insurance, indeed. Well, Fruity Puff Von Houton. We've got some important business to take care of with Mr. And Mrs. Peeps Q. Ocean Side, see?"

"Never heard of them," he says and turns to the underlings behind him. "Aye, boys, ever heard of a Peeps Q. Ocean Side?"

"We did, but he went to shit, and the hogs ate him."

"No, he's alright. HR's got him," says another.

As I break away from the conversation, my only wish is that my daughter sees the horror of this place. I hope they both do, and Ryan doesn't sell it to these people.

"Look, you guys seems like a nice family, and Christ, no, that isn't their name. I've never met the owners, but I'm sure it isn't Peeps Q."

"Alright. Carry on, soldier," says Ryan, who's begun to walk around in circles, bowlegged

71

with his thumbs in his belt loops "we best be keepin' on keepin' on, then, Chappy."

Ryan pauses, tips an imaginary cowboy hat and follows Claire back to the mirrored doors of Ocean Side's main office.

"Do you smell that?" I ask. "Back in the day when Claire was born we lived in a commune in Tempe, remember that honey, before Georgia? It smelled like this every Sunday when the trash and outhouse waste was burned."

"Thankfully, I have no recollection," says Claire with a smile as she holds the door for us.

"I couldn't wait to leave either," I tell her as I pass and smell the strawberry soap on the wind.

He saunters in, leans an elbow on the front desk and looks over at the curly-haired-Susan on the other side with a telephone strapped to her head. He is handsome up there, like an emo Frank Sinatra crossed with a straight Dean Moriarty.

"I'm Ryan Q. Peeps, and I'm here to get rich. Where do I sign?"

Susie looks up.

"Excuse me, Mr. Peeps, come again?"

"You want my land across the road. I want the check in my hand."

He lays out his palm, right under the stubble on her chin. She spots the tattoos on his arms and stiffens like she's seen an active shooter. I, however, notice the needle holes and track marks the tattoos attempt to cover. They probably fool most people, but not me. I've been trained in such things; Claire's father's arms

72

and ankles used to look the same before the
overdose took him when he was twenty, and she was
two.

"Okay, just one moment Mr. Peeps. Just one
moment."

The receptionist taps the keyboard and
whispers into her headset.

"Okay. Okay. I'll let them know," she says,
turning to Ryan with submissive eyes. "We're no
longer interested. I'm so very sorry."

"Why not?" Ryan asks.

"Cherryfield's about to auction it off to
pay for the back taxes, and the finance
department wishes to wait and purchase the land
at a tremendous discount. I wish I could do more.
I really do."

"Money fuck," says Ryan.

"A farm with a finance department?" I ask.

Susie looks around, fiddles with some
papers, takes a sip of Dr. Pepper.

"When's the auction?" asks Claire as she
crosses her arms, her bracelets jingling when
they touch.

"We're just waiting on word from the town
hall. Should be any day."

"I'm going to uppercut the town hall," says
Ryan.

"Careful, toughness," says Claire. "We'll
just go pay the tax bill and then resell it. You
can pay me back with that money."

"If you do, please come back and we will be
more than happy to continue, Mr. Peeps."

"Do you know how much is owed?" asks Claire.

"Almost seventy-five thousand," she says.

"Huh?" asks Ryan.

"Wow," says Claire. "I'm out. Sorry, Ryan."

"The property's gone up in value," she explains.

"Why?" asks Ryan, who obviously doesn't understand extrinsic value.

"Three hundred acres on Apple Ridge isn't cheap anymore. You have an ocean view up there and a whole mountain to yourself. It's probably worth ten-fold what it was bought for." Susie looks around smugly and says "rich people want to live next to seaweed and lobster. That shoots the prices up."

"How are you guys going to make any profit from such expensive land when you're only raising turkeys and pigs?" I ask.

"Besides, it's a mountain, not really the best for pasture," says Claire.

"Honey, we have dynamite, and we're subsidized. Plus, we pay a flat property tax regardless of what we own in Cherryfield, on account of the jobs we bring to this town. We always make a profit," she says with a smile.

"Can we take a tour of the farm? The barns? The animals? I'd love to see just how they live while you're making your 'profit'," I say.

"I'm sorry ma'am," says Susie, "but we don't allow tours. Our insurance bill would go through the roof if we allowed it."

"It's all about the profit," I say.

"May the demon inside you come out and purge you of your sins," says Ryan as Claire pulls him through the doors.

"We'll figure something out."

"I've got the money," I say. "I just sold the house in Georgia. It's a guaranteed payback, right?"

"Yes," says Ryan.

"No offense, new guy, but I'm asking Claire."

"Sure. They said they'd buy it."

"Alright, we'll sign a contract and go tomorrow," I tell him.

"Really?" he asks.

"Yes."

"But, you don't even know me," he says.

"I know, but I want to make these assholes pay. Besides, it's a pretty nice investment."

"Thank you."

We wait for three eighteen-wheelers to pull in then we cross the road and begin our journey back up Ruby Lane. It's one of those days when the shade requires a jacket and the sunlight, a t-shirt. I keep my coat on while Claire takes off her sweater and walks on with no shoes, wearing a baby blue Care Bears T-shirt she bought in high school.

"Will you carry me now?" asks Ryan as he drapes an arm around Claire's shoulder.

"You're not even short of breath," she says.

"Who doesn't love a piggyback, though?"

"Nobody."

"Exactly. Nobody in the history of the world."

They stop, and Claire looks up into Ryan's eyes.

"You sizin' me up, Betty?" he asks.

"Betty?"

"It's a term of endearment where I'm from," he explains.

"It's not where you're from. It's where you're at," she says, breaks the eye contact and walks on, leaving Ryan in the center of Ruby Lane, in a patch of sunlight, dumbfounded and smiling.

"I'm going to buy you some shoes," he says, jogging to catch up, "just as soon as I sell this. Some expensive ones, like Converse high tops or MJ's."

Claire continues walking but looks over her shoulder.

"I'd only put them with the others."

"It's a shame," I say.

"What is?" he asks.

"To be so insignificant as to be put with the others," answers Claire.

I kiss her cold cheek and, fourteen feet ahead, Toto wiggles on his back, legs and arms spread, in a square of sunlight that becomes momentarily darkened by the passing shadow of a swaying oak branch.

"I've never been here," I say while stepping onto the busy sidewalk.

I wait under a spindly`ficus tree and smell the city-scents of frying hamburgers and incense while Ryan finishes a cigarette. Since coming to Bangor was his idea, I follow him as he tosses the cigarette into a storm drain. Toto sprints over to retrieve it, but it's already gone. Defeated, he comes back and trots alongside us into the record shop, which, for a reason unknown to me, still exist.

Ryan goes around picking up records, flipping them, reading the track lists, then sliding the vintage square back into their milk crates for another decade. He walks by the used CD's with Toto behind him, past the used books, and starts flipping through prints in a wide box with "local artist's only" scrawled in black marker.

"Check this out," he says, holding up a beautiful print of a pond I recognize.

"That's River Pond!"

"Some of my art is still kicking around in the avenues and alleyways," he explains.

"It's beautiful. That rock across the pond is mine and Toto's favorite," I tell him.

"Mine, too."

He puts the print back into the box and shows me another of his farmhouse, only it's immaculate, beautiful, nothing of what it is today. Even the tire swing on the front lawn hangs with two children riding in it.

"I thought you didn't remember me," I say, suddenly flushed as I recognize the moment in the painting.

"I didn't have many friends," he explains, and I inch closer to him.

"So, you're famous?"

"I'm in dentist offices and shit holes."

"You're still famous. I don't care what you say. I'm glad you brought me here, still. They're wonderful."

"Let's go find some chilly air to breathe, shall we?"

"You want to know a secret?" I ask.

"Of course."

"I wrote a poem about you after that summer, my first to ever get published."

"Who printed it?"

"Highlights for Children."

Ryan looks into my eyes, cocks his head as if I'm a two-piece puzzle he's putting together.

"Can I read it?"

"I wish. I lost it a long time ago," I say, and his blue eyes sadden.

"Do you remember it?"

I shake my head.

"Maybe you'll write another," he says and steps closer to me.

"I want to see more paintings."

"I haven't painted in a long time, and I sold my last print to a guy for twenty dollars and a blow job before leaving San Francisco."

"Would you call that a liquidation?"

"I would now."

"Me, too."

"I just wanted to shoot some quick love, you know?"

"I have some paints left over from a class I taught at the Grange," I say while stepping between him and the box of prints, feeling my butt brush against his thigh, and pulling out the scene of him and me.

"I'm putting this in the living room because we are living art."

"Maybe I'll cultivate some inspiration to paint more, then," he says while we walk to the register.

"What's that?" I ask as an envelope falls from his pocket while he rummages for a lighter.

"It's the letter you wrote."

"You saved it?"

"I don't like possessions," he explains, and I don't bother to ask for the meaning, but let the idea sit like an abstract painting.

We walk outside and see our breaths. The sidewalk is filled with quick people on lunch break. Some goth kids stand in a circle on the corner, obviously cutting school to smoke cigarettes and be malnourished. To my surprise, Ryan leaves me, walks to them, looms over and asks something. I hold the print up and begin to remember that moment that existed twenty-two years ago.

"Old friends?" I ask as Ryan comes back.

"No. Just wondering if they could find something for me."

"If you want pot, I have my medical license."

"I didn't know you smoked."

"I don't. Mom wanted me to get it. She thinks it will help."

"What's ailin' ya, doll? Why do you have the card?"

"Little things. Nothing major," I tell him.

"Well, I like you, Claire. I like you a lot, and, it's not pot I'm after, but junk, heroin, monkey on my back."

"I'm sorry."

"No. I'm sorry. Sometimes I can't stop my mouth when it's hungry."

"You don't need that. It kills. Let's go home," I say.

"I could go for a blunt," he reasons.

"You and my mom can smoke one," I tell him.

"Your mom?" he asks.

"Yup."

"And you?"

"Probably not."

We walk up the sidewalk and get in my green Subaru. Toto leaps in my seat then into the back, and we drive the hour back home without talking much at first, but listening to Kesha and Iggy Azalea on the local pop station. Once the city's gone and Ryan stops threatening to twerk, we're left with peace and static only, plus the random icy tornado whenever he rolls the window down to smoke. It did make me feel good when he took the letter I wrote him from his pocket; he's a sentimental man.

28
Ryan

We got back from Bangor yesterday, and I did smoke a blunt with Claire's Mom, who, by the way, paid for the tax bill on the house, and I did forget about wanting to shoot up. Sometime around dark, Claire and Sylvia started a Gilmore Girls marathon on Netflix, and I stayed awake until the end of the first season then spent the night on the couch. I just left a couple of hours ago after Claire made pancakes, and Sylvia and I finished the blunt. My head's swimming. So much weed, so little heroin, new people that seem like old friends. New house, same as the old house. But here I am, on the road again. Don't worry Ma. It's life and life only.

Claire found me a box of acrylics and brushes and a few canvases she had left over from a class she taught at the Grange. I'd love to take a class from her. I'm pretty sure her college students loved her. She's one of those teachers that when someone asks their homegirl, "Homegirl, who'd you get for Poetry next semester?"

"Professor Claire."

"Awww, you lucky grrrl."

I sit at the kitchen table like an adult, legs crossed, back straight, hot cocoa in my hand, and look out the sliding-glass door at the green field between Claire and me. She comes out from behind her house under a maple tree with leaves the color of fresh blood. In tow is a flock of chickens chasing her down the hill while she mainlines them chicken junk in the form of corn and sunflower seeds.

I run to the bathroom, brush my teeth, rub hand soap on my pits, go back to the kitchen, grab my hot chocolate and meet Claire and her chickens by the barn.

Toto wanders under the fence that was meant to keep Dad's pigs in and sniffs the wet ground before coming back around and pawing my shin.

"How the fuck did I end up back here? I never thought I'd see another stable again," I say and lean on the fence, so I'm only a pair of lips taller than Claire.

"I dare say it's my fault. Have you started any paintings yet?"

"Your mom's coming."

"So, when are you going to paint," she asks, punching my ribs. "Stop changing the subject."

"I might take a canvas up to River Pond later on."

"Claire! Honey. Hello," says Sylvia. "Ryan, how are you feeling?"

"'Bout as good as you."

"In a cannabis coma?" asks Claire.

"Yup," says us.

"Who's that?" I ask, pointing toward the red truck turning in the dooryard.

"Well, I don't know, but who's that?" Sylvia asks, and we see a fatass pig waddling up between the house and the barn.

"Come here, piggie. Come here, girl!" The man yells while getting out of the Ocean Side truck.

Claire moves first, and we follow her until we meet the man in the field.

"What's the matter?" asks Claire.

"My sow ran away. I've come to get her."

"You've come a long way for just one pig. How many do you have down there?" asks Sylvia.

I stick out my chest and spread my arms to behold the field with two brilliant women and two dumb men, a farmhouse on either side, the peak of Apple Ridge cutting up into an empty sky and proclaim: "Who of us would not leave our flock to rescue just one lost sheep?"

"This one's tricky, this pig is," he says to Sylvia, not answering my question like a gentleman ought. "She keeps getting loose,

83

letting herself out, and I've got a fifty that says I'll keep her around long enough to eat those piglets for Thanksgiving."

"Fifty dollars?" asks Sylvia.

"Gotta feed the kids," he says "by feeding them her kids."

The pig walks up behind Claire and nips her butt.

"Ohhh!" she hollers and turns around with red cheeks.

I throw my hands in the air and nod to the snorting pig.

"Seriously?"

"What's wrong with my daughter's behind?" asks Sylvia.

"Absolutely nothing. Your daughter has the buns that I will forever compare all other buns to," I say.

"Amen to that, boy. Woooo," says the farmhand.

"Fuck off," I blurt, and he trudges through the mud betwixt us.

"Hard to believe this mountain's going to be flat as a field when we get it," he says.

I don't say anything, but chew on what this guy just said.

"What's her name?" asks Claire, breaking a moment of silence.

"Eighty-two."

The stranger moves toward the pig, who is now behind me. He grabs for her ears, and I grab his wrist.

"Hold on. I don't want any problems with you," he says.

"Why's that?" I ask, throwing back his hand.

"Let's just say you've got a reputation, and even though I think it's all pigshit, you never quite can tell. I'd rather be safe."

"I haven't been here in a decade. I don't even know you."

"Stinky shit hangs around a long time, boy," he says, walks over to the pig and hauls her by the ears back to his truck.

"That isn't necessary," Claire says, but he doesn't hear.

"How could you do that to a pregnant pig?" Sylvia hollers at him, but he's already leading her up the wooden ramp into the back of his truck.

"We should name her," says Claire while we watch the pig tied to the truck's bed fight for balance as the pickup rumbles down Ruby Lane. "Ryan. It's your job to name her. You're the creative one."

"What's wrong with eighty-two?" I ask.

"That's not a name," says Claire.

"Good a' reason as any," I oblige.

"When are you going to sell them your property?" Sylvia asks.

"I don't know. Soon?"

"Sooner or later, doesn't matter to me. I'd keep it if I could," says Sylvia.

"Sure, keep it. Just let me sleep there when it rains."

"Really?"

"I don't want it. I've got what I came for," I say.

"What's that?"

"Some clean air," I say and light a cigarette.

"I'm going to let you think about what you're saying for a couple of days."

"Okay. We should meet up later, though. I want to start painting right now. It's something about this place. It puts bubbles in my feet."

"Bubbles in your feet?"

"Bubbles-bubbles in my feet."

"Bubbles-bubbles in your feet?"

"Stop before he starts to twerk," Claire warns.

I walk back to the house, avoid the rotted step and head inside to the box Claire gave me that's in front of the fireplace. I go over, throw an armload of my parent's stuff on the fire to keep it burning, then fill my hoodie's pocket with paints and a couple of brushes. I grab a wooden palette with stains like liver spots, snatch a canvas, and go outside to head up to River Pond.

One foot off the back porch and Toto barks from up at Claire's. It echoes off Apple Ridge, making this puppy sound like a real killer. Maybe I'll call him Little Benny. Toto runs down the hill, trips, tumbles, topples, rolls, lands on his paws, and keeps on coming at a hundred all the way to my feet.

"He loves to hike," Claire hollers down from her porch.

"Especially to River Pond. He'll be your best friend," adds Sylvia.

"I'll have him back before dinner," I call up the mountain.

"Thank you," they say in unison.

"What good's a mountain that isn't being climbed?" Toto asks with electrified ears before shooting toward the trail.

29
Claire

Behind my house, a mountain shoots up straight as a gravestone to a sky whose blue hides the stars. When you look to its peak, your neck is bent as if you're catching snowflakes on your tongue. That's Apple Ridge, and on the backside is River Pond. Ryan brought Toto up here yesterday evening, and I decided to join them today. Also, there's a record high of sixty-two, and I'm celebrating by wearing a two-piece in October because, I figure, might as well while I can.

On the far shore, the opposite of where the trail ends, is a rock stretching out into the water. It's the rock from one of Ryan's paintings, the rock my mom, Toto and I slept on when we first found out I had liver cancer. This is where I lay and, on the other side of River Pond, Ryan paces along the beach with a paintbrush in his hand and a little dog following him back and forth.

I read Ethan Frome every winter; it's something I've done since I was ten. I've decided to take it off the shelf early this year, and that is what I'm doing: lying on a rock, a rolled sweater beneath my head, a blanket under my body, pretending to read while Ryan paints on the other shore. I set down Mr. Frome on the beach towel, pick up my notebook and the Sharpie and finish a

poem I was working on, then look up at a bright
sky that appears white, even though it's really
blue.

       We exist together, Ryan, Toto and I, as the
wind sets free a dying leaf above me. It shuffles
over my fingers then lands on the water, and even
though the waves fold onto this shore, the orange
leaf floats toward Ryan. I stand, dip a pink
toenail in the water, then dive in.

Claire

The dirt asked for help,
But the sky was dry.
Life's silence, however,
Grew into more
Than just a bridgeless watercourse
Painted with collusions of reds and blues.

But I asked, and naively, I ask again,
Even though I know the answer
Lies within the blank canvas
On his easel,
It is the thought before he paints.

31
Ryan

There should be a color called Johnny Cash Black. If there was, I'd use it to paint the water on the pond. Claire came up with Toto and me yesterday. It was so warm, so beautifully perfect. Today is cold, mid-thirties, and I sit next to the fire and gaze over the pond that reflects the world.

"Hey, Ryan," says Claire from behind. Toto's shotgun barks ricochet off Apple Ridge. The palette topples to the ground and all the paint's coated with sand. "I'm sorry," she says with lips that probably taste like vanilla cake.

"Jiminy Cricket. You made me squeal like Eighty-two," I say.

"Stop it. Give her a real name," she says, slapping my arm.

"Yeah. Blink Eighty-Two."

"Shush," she tells me, then bends to ruffle Toto's hair, her bracelets jingling. "How did you not hear me coming, little man?"

"Must have been daydreaming," I say.

"How's the painting going?"

"Not a damn thing, mate."

"What's the matter? You once stood in this very same spot and painted that beautiful painting you showed me at the store, which now hangs above my sofa."

I shrug and walk to where the beach meets the water. She walks next to me, and we look over to the rock we like. Toto weaves between us and slaps my shins with his wet tail.

"That's a nice fire," she says and sits in the sand next to it.

"Can I paint you?" I ask. "Check yes, no, or maybe."

"I check maybe."

"Maybe?"

"Under one condition," she says, turning to look up at me. "Please reconsider selling the land to Ocean Side. Maybe you could sell it to someone else. They do terrible things to the animals there."

"Your Mom can have it. She bought it. I even started cleaning it for her," I say then back away with the canvas and begin to paint.

"I don't think she was serious. She'd give you more money than that."

"For what?" I ask.

"To cover how much someone else would give you."

I clean the blue off my brush and dip it in orange.

"I'm glad you scared me and made me drop the pallet. The sand gives the paint a good texture."

"Lemons into lemonade," she says. "She'll seriously give you more."

"I'm rich, and I think your mom overpaid. I'll issue her a refund."

"You're an odd man, Ryan Alexander."

91

"I told her she can have it as long as I can crash there. Hobos need very little, certainly not a home. It would make a good dog house for your pooch."

"Are you a bum?" she asks.

"Of the American tradition," I say and paint the silver hoops lining the outside of her ear.

"Just what is this 'very little' that you do need?" she asks.

"Dunno. Warmth, maybe?"

"So, have you honestly not named our pig, yet?" she asks.

"I was thinking Flower."

"Why Flower?"

"Maybe she's got me twitterpated, maybe she doesn't. I don't know these things."

I darken the blue with a dab of black and paint the pond behind her.

"Flower, it is."

We spend the rest of the time in silence, me watching her watching the mountain pond. When I finish the painting, I light a cigarette and let my eyes absorb everything about her the canvas could not.

"You may move, madame."

She waits for a chickadee to finish its song before getting up. Toto gallops over from down the beach, walks to Claire's bare feet, drops a stick on them and stamps the ground, growling at her pink toenails.

32
Claire

We made it down from River Pond an hour ago, and the cold morning has become a warm evening. The air above the field between his house and mine is pale yellow and softening to gray. Suspended within it is the nose-ecstasy that is barbecued corn on the cob and Mom's garlic home fries.

"I'm going to take a shower," he had said once we made it off the mountain, and now he walks to me through the field, whistling Crazy Kids by Kesha with perfect pitch. He looks up to Apple Ridge as he walks past me sitting at the picnic table and over to Mom at the grill.

"What up, homefry?" he asks Mom and picks one off the burnt tinfoil.

"Away," she says and slaps him with a spatula.

"We should go steal Flower," he says, lighting a cigarette and sitting opposite of me.

"You mean Eighty-two?" asks Mom.

"Ayep," he says. "Sylvia, where's the gravity bong at? I wanna get high."

"I don't know what that is, but here, light this," she says and tosses him a joint. "Flower fits her beautifully."

"I don't know about stealing her. How about we just bring her an apple," I say.

"Oh, come on. It'll be fun," says Mom.

"Don't be a bird on the ground," he tells me.

"It's all about the birds with you. Isn't it?"

"I'm not sure how to answer," he confesses.

Mom puts down the spatula and looks at us over her shoulder.

"Soup's on."

Once dinner's done and the evening has become night, we leave the orb of the porch light and follow Mom and her flashlight down a dark Ruby Lane.

"I don't know about this," I say half-way down. "They said they don't want anybody there."

"Fuck dem bitches," says Ryan, laughing.

"We'll just see that she's okay then get out of there. We don't have to commit a felony tonight," Mom says while throwing an arm around my shoulder.

When we cross the empty road separating Apple Ridge from Ocean Side's and into an empty lot lit only by a few lamps, my stomach twists and clenches. There is a thudding, a throbbing, a gripping, a punching; I'm thankful nobody can see the pain in such a poorly lit place. I straighten my spine, take in a breath and relax my shoulders. I close my eyes, and when I open them, the pain has lessened, and I begin to see this place for what it is. It's a power plant, a shoe factory, a strip mall, a back-alley abortion clinic. It is not a farm.

Devoid of eighteen-wheelers and idling trucks, this animal city whispers with snorts and squeals, metal striking metal, and even though Cherryfield has less than one-thousand residents, this village is a metropolis with hundreds of thousands.

"Now what, Mom?"

"We wander. We roam."

"You're a monk," Ryan tells her.

"How are we going to find Flower, Claire?" she asks.

"Eighty-two," I say. "She's probably in the first barn with a low number like that, right?"

"My daughter is brilliant."

"She is."

Mom and I skirt around the dark side of the barn while Ryan walks to the front door, opens it, and walks in like he lives there; I don't think he knows what fear is.

A thousand, maybe two, maybe ten thousand pigs stand in rows, caged from here to the end of this windowless, fluorescent tunnel. The snorts get louder as we're recognized. Then the screaming starts, and the cage rails rattle and clang. Ten-twenty-two sees me, tries to find a corner to hide in, but there are no walls, no edges, and she can't turn around, can do nothing but stand still, big eyes shooting me, bleeding shoulders squared.

"We have to go to the last barn," I say, turning away. "These numbers are all too high. They must have the low numbers in the back. I can't look at this anymore. It's too much."

Once we're out of the steel labyrinth, the synthetic sound of exhaust rumbles up the open corridor between the barns with a searchlight preceding it. The night explodes with white light. I close my eyes, but it's too late. Blinded, I run.

"Claire!" screams Mom from behind.

"Come on. Come on. Come on," I say.

The beating of her feet keeps pace with mine as we run toward Ruby Lane and when we're near the silent road, I stop and open my eyes, but am still light-blind.

"Claire, honey. Are you okay?"

"Where's Ryan?" I ask as the army in my stomach attacks again.

"I don't know. I don't know."

I turn around and hug my stomach.

"Oh, dear. We need to find him," says Mom.

We run back to the barn in time for the truck to start, and to be shot again with the spotlight. It drives away in a wake of exhaust fumes and redneck laughter.

Once they're gone, only the rattling of cages can be heard. I lean against the barn's metal shell, still unable to see, and press my ear to it and listen to the cage rails clang over and over and over until my eyes adjust to the night again.

"Mom, there he is."

"Where? I still can't see."

"Over there, on the ground."

33
Ryan

I want to kill them. If my shotgun wasn't swimming with the lobsters in Casco Bay, it would've been shot by now, splattering heads like they be Gallagher's watermelons. I'm thankful to past Ryan for chucking it. You can't kill too close to home, you know? I hear It'll give you a shitty reputation. Still, getting my ass kicked took away the need to shoot up; It was pretty and thrilling.

Ten stitches slice down my eyebrow. The skin below my ribcage is bruised to the point it looks burnt. There's a pressure behind my temples that makes me wish they'd had the balls to kill me, but I'm grateful they didn't, especially on a day like today. I feel something emotional, something alien, something that made waking up this morning seem like less of a decision between suicide and emptiness and more like something inevitable, continuous, planned, that should be enjoyed for the price of zero dollars and maybe some change. I take a handful of aspirin, finish this joint and answer the door.

34
Claire

"I brought a rope for the tire swing," I
say while tilting my head up at the pink sky
above his house. "I thought you could use a
little cheering up."

"So you brought me a noose?" he asks,
admiring my craftsmanship.

"I was going to hang myself, but that can
wait. Let me look at you. Step out here," I say
as I inspect his handsome face. "The swelling's
gone down. That scar is going to be hot as hell."

"Word," he says and snatches the noose from
me.

Ryan hurries off the steps, to the base of
the tree, next to the old tire. He throws the end
of the rope over the same branch it used to hang
from, beside the old knot, and pulls the rope's
end down. Ryan rolls the tire off the tree, picks
it up and balances it on his knee. I take the
rope, weave it through the hole and tie it
together, so the tire hangs a couple of feet from
the ground.

"Now what?" he asks.

"I'm not sure. Swing it?"

We push the tire back and forth under a sky
the color of cotton candy, listening to the last

few insects of the year chirping in the cool evening.

"One night, when we were on our way to see Gram, we stopped at Storyland. It was the summer you and I met. That sky was the same color."

"It was beautiful then?"

"Exactly the same color as the strawberry milkshake Mom and I shared," I say and stop the tire from swinging. "This isn't right. We're riding this. Hop in."

"Okay."

"You first," I say and push the swing into his hands.

"I like the way your bracelets sound when they clang together. It's like I'm Pavlov's dog."

I wiggle my wrists so the bracelets jingle then catch the tire he's pushed back.

"I've worn them for so long, I don't even notice anymore. Get in," I say.

"I don't even remember how. I'm going to fall on my face."

"Just close your eyes, forget the world and stick in your feet."

Ryan stretches one long leg through, then he holds the rope and slides the second in. I go behind him, place my palms on his back and push as we look out, beyond the house and barn, to the pasture where the first rocks of Apple Ridge jut out from the wilting grass. Ryan holds onto the rope with both hands and leans all the way back so he can see up my nose.

"Get in," he says.

"Get out, then."

"No."

"What do you mean 'no'?"

"You didn't make me get out when we were five, and you're not going to do it now," he claims.

"I don't remember that, but fine."

"It'll be fun."

"I know it will," I say as I hold the rope above his head while swiveling around so our eyes meet. He sticks out his hands. I grab them, feeling his fingers close around mine. I put one leg into the hole, then the other and slide onto his lap, the tire between us. I wrap my fingers around his which hold the rope and we rock in lazy circles in an autumn air caught somewhere on the later side of evening. I squeeze his hands, and the motion light flickers on, telling us it's now dark, but it shows me something, something in his eyes, something new, like the eyes of a child just born.

"Hello, Claire," he says.

"Hello, Ryan."

35

Claire

After the night at Ocean Side, and the pain I felt during, I made an appointment, and I've just arrived home from the doctor's office with a ticket for my final departure; the cancer is growing, they say.

"How did the appointment go? I wish you would have let me come," Mom says as I sit with her at the kitchen table.

"Just a checkup. No need to bother. All is well."

"Great, honey. That's wonderful."

"Sure is."

A smile grows on Mom's face, and her eyes widen. Her neck tilts a little to the left causing the gray hair behind her ear to fall to her shoulder.

"Now that the important stuff is out of the way, is Ryan answering the door? I hope he's not dying of internal bleeding," she says.

I grab the cribbage board from the window sill and pause as I spot the photo of Ryan and me; yesterday I sat on that same tire. I smile, shuffle the cards and look out the window at the smoke coming from Ryan's chimney.

"He's perfect," I say.

"Oh?"

"Yep."

Mom lights the bowl and passes it to me, which, for the second time in my life, I happily take, inhale, cough, deal out the cards and cough again.

"Honey, you've got to take it easy. I've been at it since the seventies."

"I'll get better, Mom. I promise" I say, take another hit and pass back the bowl.

"Practice, practice, practice," she says.

"Fifteen, two," I counter.

"A pair is three."

"Mom, look. Snow."

"Beautiful."

I wince and wrap my arms around my stomach.

"Oh, God, it hurts."

Pain claws and climbs my spine. In my head, something recites "Tic-toc. Tic-toc. Tic-toc. Tic-toc."

"Claire, are you okay?"

I put down my cards, grip my thighs and breathe as pain rips chunks of life from my storehouse.

"We should go outside. I could use some snow," I say, and open my prescription bottle, taking out a single pill. I swallow it and enter the outdoors wearing a tank top and shorts.

Ryan walks onto his back porch and sits on the steps with a canvas on his knees. I sit in a wicker rocking chair and look down the field, through thin layers of falling snow, to the copper weathervane spinning on his barn's peak.

36
Ryan

Today, it snows slowly, but they're big, fat flakes. Toto yips and jumps down the hill toward me, but stops to bite at the snow and turns around.

Claire's out on her porch, too, and I think of Nicole and how I should care more about leaving her, but this is a different world, over here. It couldn't be further away, at least in my mind, from California, and I feel better for it.

I put a canvas on my lap and paint. I focus on Claire's house, the snowy roof, and the mountain behind it with its gray edges striking out from blankets of white and pillows of green.

There's a maple to the left of her house with snowy boughs, from which hangs a single swing with a mound of snow on the seat. I imagine Claire sitting on it, swaying in the diagonal snowfall.

I finish the painting, hold it up to get a better look then set it down, leaning it against the railing. Claire steps off her porch and into the snow, wearing only beach gear and walks toward me. As soon as Toto sees where she's going, he shoots in my direction, but Claire turns and walks back up the hill to her home, taking with her Toto and my hope for an enjoyable day. Her head is down; she's probably studying the prints her bare feet made on the way down.

37
Claire

The air is dry, the snow beautiful, and my barefoot path down to Ryan's resembles the trail on a child's treasure map. I tried to go there during the snowfall, but my liver hurt worse than ever. I wasn't going to take many of the pills, but I changed my mind this morning when I realized how miserable this disease can be. There's just no other way to deal with the pain. As a straightedge girl high on pot and opiates, I'm finally kind of enjoying cancer. Not really, but kind of. Regardless, I can see where this is going, so I've made another appointment with the doctor to get a higher dosage.

It's beginning to swell, my stomach is. Mom can't see it, yet, but I can. There's also a pressure where there wasn't pressure before, like the pressing out of a rotten apple from underneath my ribcage.

"Would you like another cup of coffee," Mom asks.

"No, I'm fine. Thanks, though."

"Hey, honey. Are you going to see Ryan?"

I get up, stand behind her, place my elbows on the back of her chair and try to read the faded letters on her book's pages.

"Yeah, sometime soon. I miss him."

"Already?"

"Already. I want to see Flower, too. I've been worrying about her all the time."

"Me, too. We should go."

I sit back in my chair and look over the snowy canopy below Ryan's house and to the black Atlantic Ocean where, somewhere, it becomes only a horizon, where nothing further exists.

We do this for most of the day: talking, drinking coffee, reading. In the afternoon, Mom and I get something to eat then talk about nothing again until sunset, when, after locking up the chickens for the night, we decide to visit Flower.

I zip my coat, tuck my chin underneath the scarf and tug a blue knit hat over my ears, go outside and get in Mom's car.

"Ready?" she asks.

"Ready," I say.

"We should let Ryan heal for the night."

"I agree. Just you and I."

She drives slow down Ruby Lane. Ryan's lights are on, and I find his shadow in an upstairs window. Once we're near the end of Ruby Lane, she drives a little way with the lights off before shutting off the engine.

"Ready?"

"Ready."

We each take a deep breath and walk into the field beside the parking lot.

"It's weird without Ryan," I say.

It takes us a half hour to sneak to the last barn where, presumably, Flower is. We open the front door, and the smell is unbelievable, way worse than the first barn. It's like if you cooked spaghetti in outhouse waste.

It's quiet, the pig's bedtime, but the lights are on. I don't see or hear a heater anywhere amid the clanging of cloven hooves on loose grates and the ringing of cage rails, but the place is warm and damp from swine breaths. They can't move in their gestation crates, can't turn around, can't scratch their itches. Mom walks down one lane, and I walk another.

"Sixty-one, sixty-four," she counts. "We're in the right place."

They gnaw at the rails caging them; down these aisles is a supermarket of submission. I see her head first, as a pig walks around the corner and trots down the aisle, snorting like a happy dog, the grated floor shifting under her and me. I run my hand along her spine and feel the scars from her having too much energy for a coffin.

"Did you let yourself out again?"

"That's her. Look at the fresh cuts," Mom says, coming over.

"What do we do?" I ask as I check the number tattooed on her ear.

"I don't know, honey."

She kneels next to me and rubs Flower's pregnant, drooping stomach.

"They said they'd kill her if she got out again," she says.

106

A truck pulls up outside the barn, and a
door shuts.

"What do we do?" I ask.

"We need to put her back and sneak out
somehow."

"Put her back? Look at her," I say and rest
my temple on Flower's cheek.

"They'll kill her and her babies if she's
out. You heard them."

We walk back the way Flower came but don't
ask her to follow. She does anyway, waddling and
snorting. We turn the corner, and there's an open
crate with *eighty-two* written on a placard.
Flower stops.

"They'll kill you, honey," Mom says.
"They'll kill you."

"Please, just go in," I beg.

She doesn't understand; she's a pig, a pig
with hauntingly understanding eyes. We get behind
Flower and push until she chooses to waddle in. I
close the gate, and Mom snaps the lock. Flower's
eyes meet might as she nudges the metal rail with
her snout.

"Let's go out the back," says Mom as the
front door opens.

"Stop forgetting to shut these lights off,
dip shit," says one as the place goes dark.

We crouch and wait for the door to close
and the truck to take off before leaving. Once
outside, we run and don't stop until Ruby Lane.

"We need to get her," Mom says once she
catches her breath.

"We do."

38
Ryan

It's night. It's cold, and I'm in my old bedroom, still trying to rest and heal from that glorious beatdown. As many times as I quit drugs, I never get used to the niceness of sobriety. Drugs are a blast, but seeing the world with pure vision offers something of itself, too, mainly clarity.

I get off the bed and walk around the room. I had a rocking horse which sat in the corner by the closet. It was ridden to hell by Raggedy Anne and Andy, never by me. It was next to the bookshelf Mom made me for my tenth birthday, which is still there, beside the window. She put First Meditations and Catcher in the Rye on it, along with bookends she made with two rocks from River Pond.

This is the room of someone else, though, someone I am not. It's the setting from a movie I once knew by heart but have since forgotten. There's still a little blood in the crack of the wooden floor beside my bed from Dad; to anyone else it's a stray line of paint. The police took the comforter and the pillow, but some of the red leaked through onto the mattress. Sometimes I miss Dad, but then I see this, and that feeling's gone.

I open the window, and a breeze comes in through the darkness, a breeze which is a detail of the past I remember. The house is warm, but the wind is cold. It smells like cooking food, like bread, or muffins, like Sylvia is making something delicious up on the hill.

There's a knock at the door.

I leave my room, go out onto the balcony and look over the banister at the front door.

"Come on in," I say as I slide down the railing.

Claire walks in, and I hug her, burying my mouth into the frost on her blue wool hat. She takes off her mittens and rubs her palms together.

"Hello, Mr. Alexander."

"Hello, Claire."

She takes off her scarf and her jacket, puts them on the back of the couch. I go to the pile of Dad's stuff by the fireplace and throw in a leather belt, some letters, and the syringe and spoon I've been carrying around this whole time.

"Do you want something to eat, or drink?" I ask.

"No, thanks. I don't have much of an appetite."

"Not feeling well?" I ask as I sit on the floor.

She wraps her arms around her waist and we watch the sparking fireplace.

"Yeah, but it's not contagious," she says.

I scoot back and lean my shoulders against the couch. Claire sits on the cushion behind me.

"I like your socks," I tell her.

"Thanks. I knitted them."

"You're an amazing lady."

"So, Mom and I went to see Flower. She let herself out of the cage."

"No way. What did you do?"

"The guys came back, and so we locked her in and ran. Your face is healing well."

"The scar will be nice," I assure her.

"I'll take the stitches out in a few days."

"Thank you."

Claire gets off the couch and sits with me on the floor.

"We need to get her, Ryan. It's so bad in there. The pigs can't move. They have no room. They chew on steel bars all day. It's terrible. They should be climbing mountains and eating mud."

"Eating mud?"

"Sure, why not?"

"Let's do this. Fuck it, I say."

"You say?"

"I say."

She jumps up, slips on the hardwood floor and falls on me. Claire looks down, and I look up.

"Your breath smells like Bubblicious," I say.

"I haven't had that since I was a kid."

She gets up, but her ghost presses into me.

"Want to see my bedroom?"

"I'm not that kind of girl, Mr. Alexander."

"Not like that. There's nothing amazing up there, except me. It's just cool to see where someone grew up, what they were like before the world fucked them.

39
Claire

Once at the top of the stairs, on my way to Ryan's bedroom, I hold onto the banister. My pores open, and I now know that I've swallowed too many painkillers. I haven't taken this many before, so now I know my limit. Even minutes ago, this opiate-feeling was bliss, but my body has plummeted to hell.

There's a tugging on my stomach, then down the skin enlisted to protect my ribs. Needles prod the pores and don't stop ratcheting, bringing with each jab seaworthy-nausea and gunshots. I rest my elbows on the banister then slide down until my butt's on the floor.

My throat is tight, and the sweat is cold. A wave knocks me over, pulsing throughout this body the way an octopus swims: contract and spread, contract and spread. Trying to understand this life is carrying a lighter to melt a glacier.

I grip the banister, but my hands shake too much. Ryan puts his on mine to steady them. My tendons are limp rope, frayed to the last few threads. The space within my skin is an attic, and it chokes on the floating spores, and it is now that I realize opiates are worm holes for metaphors.

"Here. Come over here," Ryan says as he puts his hands on my hips and helps me back so that I'm steady against the wall. "I'll be right back with some water."

When he returns, we sit for a while longer, sipping water, smoking a joint and eating sugar cookies, my favorite, with our backs against the wall. The white balusters rise like jailhouse bars.

"Are you high on opiates?" he asks.

"Painkillers," I say.

"Claire, I'm a junky. You could hide a bag anywhere on Apple Ridge and I'd sniff it out within twenty-four hours."

"Painkillers from the doctor," I say as headlights light up the downstairs windows.

"Who's that?" he asks.

"It's not my house," I remind him.

"Is it your Mom?"

"Maybe, but she'd likely walk. You don't have any idea of who it might be?" I ask.

"I have a hunch."

A car door slams and rattles the front window. High heels slam into the frozen porch wood. There is no knock, only an opening door and a dark-haired model. She steps onto the stairs, and I realize this is someone he's familiar with. We stand, and I wait for Ryan to take a few steps before following him down the stairs.

He calls her "Nicki", and she calls him "baby".

"I fly in to surprise you and you've got someone else here? What the fuck, Ryan? Who is this slut?" she asks. "Is she the reason you won't be with me?"

I tilt my head and try to understand the reasoning in something so irrational.

"Why would you call me that?"

"Nicole, go in the kitchen. I'm sure you're hungry. I know how much you hate airplane food."

"I flew first class. The food was great."

"I'll get your bags, and then we'll talk," he says to her.

She turns and walks into the kitchen. Ryan turns to me, but I go around him and get my coat and scarf from the back of the couch. I put them on and pull my hair out from under the collar.

My liver is a thin-walled heart, and it beats, and it tears.

"I guess this is goodbye, then," I say.

"I'm sorry. It's not what you think. Seriously. I've never slept with her," he says as if that disqualifies love.

She calls from the kitchen: "Ryan, get my bags, please. We should order pizza tomorrow. Is there any place to eat in this shit town?"

"I know what you're thinking," he whispers.

"That she's going to throw up that pizza?"

This makes him laugh.

113

"Please stay," he says.

"No, that's fine. We'll meet up later."

I walk out the door that she hadn't shut. There are a trillion stars out, and the glowing Milky Way cuts through the center of the sky like surgical hose wrapped around a bicep.

Everything is a shade of gray, from the light curves of the field to the dark forest walls, and the medium tone of the mountains. Their colors lie somewhere on the gray-scale between the blowing brightness of a burning star and the darkness surrounding it.

The wind sounds different when it's frozen; it's sharp, and when it whistles, it's higher pitched, like if you could hear frozen saltwater screaming.

The trees sound different, too. Most of the leaves have fallen, so instead of hearing them shimmer upon the branch, you hear the wind stuttering as it's numbed by thick evergreen boughs, or as it shoots through naked limbs, making them rattle like bones.

Then there are the leaves, the dried, crumbly things, like mummy's skin. On the ground, they are scurrying cockroaches; between my toes and the frozen dirt, they are the fracturing of a mockingbird's wings, and I realize that they will soon be the shingles on my forever-home.

When I get to the house, Mom is in the living room, sitting on the couch and watching television. I hang my coat and scarf on the coat rack and pull the wool hat with the white snowflakes over my ears. I walk through the

kitchen and into the living room, sit on the
couch and lay down so my head is on Mom's lap.
She strokes my hair as we watch Party of Five.
"Mom," I say.
"Yes, honey?"
"I think I like Ryan."
She tucks my hair behind my ear and runs
her hand down my arm.
"I know you do."

40
Claire

Mom and I sit, drinking coffee on the porch
while Toto and the chickens kick around dirt and
snow in the driveway. Since the doctor put me on
painkillers, Mom's been forced to make twice as
much coffee as before just to keep me awake.
Being high is nice, though, and it's easy to see
why Mom and Ryan like to be there; it's an oasis
in a sullied desert, the casket at a funeral.
It's happiness in an unhappy place.
I wonder, what about that minute before
death, will I contemplate a future?, or will I be
in such a panic as to have my last sixty seconds
be crushed by fear and shaking panic? Will there

be time to react? Time to know? The pills and pot turn it into a game, the fear and fortune-telling of living and dying, as if we're not all terminal. What's behind door number one, Claire? I choose number three.

"Take the fire exit," says my brain.

When I was studying poetry in Georgia, I never would have thought I could have, one day, wanted death to feel like marijuana and opiates. I can count the times I've had alcohol on one hand with fingers left over, but I find that drugs disintegrate sadness and loneliness, and I'm okay with disintegrating.

I understand that this "I" is nothing but a placeholder, that every atom of my body and mind was once something else entirely. I try not to get too philosophical about the whole thing, since it would be easier for a chair to understand the carpenter than it would be for me to understand *why* the universe would create something only for its progeny to say, "Wow, you're awesome". It is conceited, but it's a beautiful gift. Thank you, Universe, from the bottom of my liver.

"What are you thinking, honey," asks Mom as she looks over from her patio chair.

"Making plans for the week."

I swallow a mouthful of coffee.

"Ahhhh!" I say as it burns my tongue and heats my body.

"Chill, baby, chill," she says. "We should get Ryan and make a plan to rescue Flower. I've been thinking about it, and we can easily hide her in his barn."

"His new friend, though."

"I'll slap her if she says something to you."

"No violence."

I appreciate Mom's gusto, and that, too, warms me.

"Fine."

"Mom. It's no big deal. I just don't know how interested he'll still be in saving Flower with a guest."

"She's nothing."

"As are you. As am I."

"Give me back the joint," she says, laughing. "You've had too much."

Mom holds the cup in her lap with both hands while the smoldering joint dangles between her fingers. I grab it.

"Claire, let's go for a walk then." She stands up, not commenting on the events of joint stealing that have come to pass. "Come on."

"I don't want to go there, Mom."

"We won't. Come on. Just a little walk, work these leg of ours, give Toto a little exercise. I need to rest this book, anyway," she says as she folds a page corner in Anna Karenina and stands up.

"You've almost finished."

"Only a few hundred pages left."

She spreads her arms across the snowy world, embracing Ryan's farmhouse, the sloping mountain and the Atlantic Ocean beyond.

117

"You're right. The sun is bright, and the breeze is special. Let's go," I say.

"As you wish."

"Be right back."

I run to my bedroom, put on blue jeans, roll up the cuffs, and slip into a sweater. I wrap my hair behind my head, clip it, find the wool socks I wore yesterday and pull those on, too. A pill goes in my mouth, then I go downstairs to a cute little Toto, who sits at the door and lifts his paw to beckon me outside.

I wait for Mom to wrap a scarf around her neck, and then we begin our walk.

"When do you want to get Flower?" Mom asks as we leave the driveway.

"I think we'll have to do it without Ryan."

"She's Irrational. A bitch. I bet if you ask Ryan why she's here, he couldn't give you an answer. He had no idea she was coming, right?"

"Right."

"And he wasn't happy to see her?"

"Didn't seem so," I say.

"Then she's a nut, and he needs a quiet minute to shove her off without hurting her feelings too badly."

Toto barrels into the snow and runs to Ryan's back lawn.

"Toto, get back here," I say, going into the snow after him.

He sniffs the ground, circles, walks in further, stops, squats and poops. Mom laughs. I laugh, then Toto and I meet her again on the road.

"I'm not mad at him, Toto, but thanks for the gesture," I say and rub the coarse hair on his head.

"They're outside," Mom says.

Nicole stands behind Ryan on the stairs, draping her arms down his shoulders and rubbing her breasts on the back of his head.

He sees us and shakes her off. Mom waves. I wave. He waves.

"Hold on," says Mom and walks up Ryan's driveway.

I stand next to the rusted mailbox, waiting for Mom, and look down Ruby Lane for Toto.

"Hi, Claire," he calls.

I turn and wave again.

"Hello," I say as Mom speaks with them before coming back.

"She is pretty," Mom says, "but Ryan doesn't like her."

"It's fine. Let's go, shall we?"

A minute later, Toto sprints to us, stops at my feet for a head rub, then he's off again, disappearing around a corner.

"So, when's the next doctor's appointment?" she asks.

I still haven't told her I got my death date.

"Monday," I say.

"Monday," she says.

We meet up with Toto and walk to the end of the road where Ruby Lane meets Route 1. Ocean Side is busy, trucks coming and going, carrying animals whose pink, snorting noses poke out

119

between snow-lined railings to sniff frozen, sixty mile per hour wind. When I was helping to watch over Gram, I hadn't realized just how bad of a place this is. It always appeared too industrial for a farm, but it was still a farm, and most carry charm; I saw only the image on the package.

My liver spasms, and I fall to my knees. Gravel cuts into my skin, and I try to catch my breath. Mom panics, rubs my backs, says many things as I try to calm her. I begin to breathe steadily and stand up but can't keep my knees straight. Toto places a paw on my big toe and looks into my eyes.

"I'm coming," I say and rub his head.

That apparently satisfies him, because he's off again, running just as fervently uphill as he had on the way down.

By the time we get home, I am so absent of energy that I collapse on the couch, but the sun is in my eyes, so Toto and I go upstairs to my bedroom. I roll on my side, pull the sheet to my chin, and he goes under, curling into the space behind my knees.

"Toto, how much longer will I feel the push of your tiny, warm breaths on my skin?"

When I die and if Toto dies and we are buried in the same vicinity, and our molecules mingle, and we become food for a night crawler, then the night crawler becomes food for a partridge, and then the partridge becomes a meal for Mom, we will then become her, too. Maybe my molecules and Toto's mix with Mom's consciousness molecule, and we three will hang out in her wheelhouse. I think about telling Mom that Toto and I may one day become her, but I don't want her wasting her life away killing the tranquil graveyard birds.

I grab the pill bottle off the nightstand, take three, which is two more than I'm prescribed, move a little closer to Toto, pet him under the covers until the meds calm me, then pray to no one in particular that my final life's minute be as pleasant as this.

41

Ryan

Nicole's gone to find dinner in Bangor, and I've decided to pick up the window cleaner and paper towels. I wipe the last window pane in my father's room and am almost done cleaning Sylvia's house. In this room, there is a closet, and in that closet hangs the final piece of trash: a green jean jacket camouflaged with blood. That's the jacket Dad wore the last time he beat Mom and me. I hung it in the closet before the police came to take the body.

All the blood on it's not his; some is my mother's from the final time he beat her, just before he called the police to tell them she fell from the cliff on Apple Ridge. When they showed up, they had two bodies; double suicide they said. Dad even took her up there on his shoulder and pitched her off the edge while I sat on the tire swing.

I take the jacket from the hanger, sling it over my shoulder and walk out onto the balcony, then to my room. I light a cigarette and open the window by my bed. The cliff above Claire's house is oddly bright, releasing all its light like it's a mirror. Claire's wearing white today, the sun reflecting off her, as well, as she sits on the rocky edge. She is a dot, a micro-machine, but it is her; I know those curves, her unique shape.

I run downstairs, put the jean jacket into the fireplace, then go to the kitchen where my art supplies are. I tuck a canvas under my arm, fill my hands with paints, paintbrushes, and the wooden palette, then go outside on the back porch as she walks away from Apple Ridge.

I sit on the steps and paint the memory, using the smallest brush and taking my time on every curve as I paint her looking out from the mountain's edge, just as she was. When the painting's finished, a voice tells me it's Claire that's beautiful, and not the paint. I hear Nicole's rental car coming up Ruby Lane, her door opens and shuts, then she's talking on a phone. I go in and meet her in the living room.

"Thank you. We'll be here," she says into the cell phone. "Yes. That's right, me and my fiance." She pauses and winks at me. "Yes, I understand that he has to be here to sign the papers. I'll make sure of it."

She hangs up and stuffs the phone into the pocket of her leather jacket.

"Ryan," she says. "We have a buyer! Ocean Side's going to pay a premium now."

"What do you mean? There is no 'we', and I'm not selling this place to those people. How did you even talk to them?"

"They met me at the bottom of the hill and asked me to let you know," she says. "I gave them my number and some guy called before I made it up here. What's the matter? Isn't that why you came here, to get rid of this for big cash?"

"It was."

"Then what's changed?" I don't say a thing. "It's Claire, right?"

"Hold on," I say and stare into the fire, at the ashes of the bloody jean jacket.

"Well, what's the problem?" she asks.

My brain floats on ice water.

"Ryan, are you listening to me?"

I shake my head and walk to the staircase.

"Ryan," she calls.

I stop and put my hand on the banister.

"I can't do it," I say

"Can't do what?"

"This. You're a great friend, but you need to leave."

I walk up the rest of the stairs, bang a right, then down to my bedroom.

"No! I don't need to leave. What's gotten into you?" she asks while running up the stairs. I meet her at the top.

"I can't be with you. I can't love you."

"Why?"

"Because of love someone else."

She lights a cigarette, follows me into my room then picks up my copy of Catcher in the Rye off the bookshelf, flips the orange cover, then puts it back. She looks out the window that opens to the backyard and Claire's house and flicks her cigarette out.

"You've been painting?" she asks.

"Yeah. It doesn't matter, though. You need to leave," I say.

"Where is it? I want to see it," she says.

"Why?" I ask and sit down on the edge of the bed.

"Nevermind. I'll leave," she says.

42
Claire

Mom sits beside me on the bed. Toto buries himself under the covers and curls up by my hip.

"Do you want another damp towel?" she asks.

"No, that's okay," I say. "I'm getting cold again."

"Okay. I'll get one. You'll need it in a minute," she says and gets up.

I ran a fever last night, a half-degree below the one I have this morning. I'm freezing, but I'll be boiling by the time Mom comes back with the washcloth. I've been naked for two days in an attempt to regulate my temperature, but I do finally feel okay.

I scoot back to the headrest, not caring that my breasts are out. I put the plate of toast and peanut butter Mom brought me for breakfast on my lap.

"So, kind of taken a turn for the worst?" she asks as she comes in with a glass of ice water.

"Yes," I say.

She sits on top of the covers. Toto scurries up and sticks his head out from under the blanket.

"You'll get better. I know it," she says.

"Will you pass me a t-shirt?" I ask.

"Why? You're burning up, honey. I can feel your legs on fire through the blanket."

"I'm cold again."

She gets up, opens the second drawer of my dresser and brings me a gray Georgia University T-shirt.

"Mom."

"Yes, doll?"

"I'm not going to get better."

"What? Of course, you are."

"You know how I had that doctor's appointment the other day?" I pause to look around the room. "You know how I just flipped the calendar to October?" She stares into the needle points within my eyes. "That will probably be the last time I change months."

We lay in bed, not talking. Downstairs, the television plays reruns of fake studio laughter.

"Are you hungry?" she asks.

"No, but I'd still like to eat. I'm feeling better," I say. "This peanut butter toast isn't doing it for me."

"I'll make some french toast."

I get out of bed and stand in front of the mirror. I'm thinner, but my stomach's showing the bloat caused by my failing liver. I go to my dresser and take out a pair of yoga pants and pull them on.

I wonder what Flower is doing right now. No doubt she is in that gestation crate if she's still alive. I thought they would have given her something bigger, at least while she's pregnant.

My skin begins to roast, so I open the windows behind my bed and stick my head out the right one. It's got to be forty degrees, or so, and the air feels great on my sweaty body. Finally, I am cooled, or was I already cold?

Snow summersaults down from a gray sky. I turn my head to the clouds and open my mouth, feeling a cottony snowflake dissolve on my bottom lip.

"Claire, honey," Mom calls from downstairs.

"Yeah?"

"Ryan's here."

"Be right down." I close the windows, go to the mirror and realize that bedhead might work for me.

My liver throbs, and I reach for the yellow bottle with the magical pain pills. One small white one, the shape of a full moon, falls onto my palm; that is the prescribed dosage. Two more happen to fall,

then one more. The four feel good together,
and for a moment, I imagine they were
friends in their other life, the life in the
orange bottle. To do anything to split them
up would be a crime against love, so I put
the foursome in my mouth and swallow, clip
my hair behind my head and go downstairs.

43
Ryan

On account of being a junky and all, I
wanted some heroin, so I took Claire for a
ride to Bangor. She felt like shit, so I
drove. I never told her I was taking the
trip to find drugs, but I'm sure she knows.
She's just like that: omnipotent,
infallible, and these are the reasons I love
her.

Now that we're here, shivering on a
park bench, I don't want drugs. I mean, I
want it, but I don't want-want it. Back in
the day, I'd do anything just this side of
swallowing for a bag, but now it's
different, absent of passion.

We sit in Pickering Square on a bench below a tree planted by a hypothetical guy we named Guy, who sucked down Pall Mall's and Mt. Dew while watching young runaways, bums, and wannabe monks from the corners of his eyes. Guy's made up, true, but this nutty bastard tweaking on the curb is for real.

In front of Titty Humpers, Stephen King's strip joint, stands a sixty-year-old man in torn suspenders, a gray beard and a crooked hat which he keeps taking off and putting back on as he chats with a busted police radio and kicks a mound of brown snow.

There's this look on his face that screams importance. His face is frazzled, pensive, serious, significant, horny, pondering, then his eyes snap to the top of the Fleet Building like he's found the answer, which he probably has.

People need him. The world needs him, this he makes obvious by huffing and yelling, taking his hat off and putting it back on, yet he comes here, such an important man, to a city square filled with people that could disappear and it's likely nobody would give a shit. It's us, though, the forgettables of the world, he wants to remember him.

"What do you think about that man?" Claire asks as she moves closer to me on the bench.

Her hand is on her thigh, and I put mine on top. There's a soft pressing on my shoulder as she lays her cheek on it.

"He's the greatest American hobo ever to exist."

"I think so, too," she says. I lean to put my lips on the top of her head but pull back as soon as a soft hair tickles them. "So, why did you want to come to Bangor?" she asks.

"I forget," I say and put my arm around her shoulders, my temple on her head, and we continue watching the God made flesh flipping his hat around and around in front of King's jerk off hut.

"Repeat! Repeat! Repeat! I do not copy. Take the left. The Left!" he screams at the radio, then throws it to the ground, stomps, and trudges up to Main Street saying the nastiest shit that makes me blush.

Claire wedges under my arm and curls into my rib cage.

"Ryan, I'm dying soon."

I try to talk, but my lungs are a vacuum: nothing in, nothing out.

44

Claire

Ryan and I went to Bangor yesterday,
and he explained the Nicole situation a
little better, and I explained the cancer
situation a little better. We had a moment
on a bench in a busy city, and it was
enjoyable.

I don't know why I'm thinking so much
about this man and so little about my
health, my chickens, my mother, Toto, the
students that I've left behind. I very well
may have less than a month left here, so why
care about anything? I suppose that even
though the body dies, love and longing
cannot.

The doctor said the pain is only going
to worsen. It's not constant, but when it
comes it's like all my nerves are being
shredded with a bread knife.

I've spent all day swallowing pills,
taking the occasional hit with Mom, and
thinking about Flower. Today's going to be
in the mid-forties so, to celebrate this
gift of warmth, I'm in shorts and a tank
top, lying on a foldout chair that's planted

in the crusty snow where Apple Ridge becomes my back lawn.

The wind blows between my toes, up my shins, my torso then washes over my face. It tosses a few wisps of hair into the air and then nothing, a lull, and I hear Ryan and Nicole fighting again.

I hadn't been able to understand anything, not until they came outside. Mom waves from the porch. I wave back, and she gestures toward Ryan's house.

"Because I love her," he says.

"You were serious?" she hollers and points to my house.

"That's why you need to leave. You're a great friend, a wonderful person, but you're only in the way."

Mom walks toward me, trudging through the narrow path in the snow I made on the walk over.

"So, I hear you've got an admirer," she says while shading her eyes.

"I guess so."

"What now?" she asks.

"We swing," I say as Mom passes me a joint, and I take a couple of drags then give it back.

"You shouldn't be smoking," Mom says.

It takes a second for her to realize the irrationality of her statement and then gives me the joint. I prop myself up on my elbows.

"I never thought I'd be a drug fiend," I say.

"Oh, honey, you're so not a drug fiend. Look."

Mom gestures down the hill as Nicole's car spits snow and gravel while leaving the driveway.

Ryan sits on his porch steps and puts a large canvas on his lap.

I wonder why I like him; I wonder if I've always liked him. Perhaps this is why people enjoy hospices and retirement homes. We're all going to die, whether it's in a week and a day, or only two hours, but even as death waits a measurable amount of sunsets away, we all search for the same thing; love.

Not just romantic love, but friendship love, companionship love. I reach down and stroke Toto's back, who's lying happily in the snow. He looks up at me, panting. We live for our love of a fried egg and peanut butter toast, for the coffee that washes it down. We live for our love of music. We live for the chance of love, even just a chance. We live for our love of October air at six in the morning, the smell of a Christmas

133

house packed with family. We live for our own reasons, yet they are everyone's.

"I'll be right back," I say to Mom.

I push off the chair, go to the house and walk down the pathway Ryan and I dug. Toto runs ahead then leaps into the snowbank. A pain explodes in my stomach. I clench my teeth, breathe in broken glass, and continue.

I sit next to Ryan on the steps before saying a word. He reaches down and ruffles Toto's hair as he squeezes between us. I peek over at the canvas and see me, my mother, and Toto all lying at the base of a snowy Apple Ridge.

"Are you going to make me famous, Mr. Alexander?"

"I think you're going to make me famous."

He turns and watches me, not in the way an artist sees their subject, but the way my face gets at the sight of spring's first butterfly. I tell Ryan I'm going for a walk. He asks if he can join me, but I point to the canvas and say, "Sorry, you've got to stay here and make us famous."

Toto stays with him, and I walk away, slowly creating my path in the snow while skirting around the backside of the house to the driveway. I walk to where the forest

meets the lawn, sit on a big, gray rock and
watch the snow-covered tire swaying in the
breeze.

The branches above me are all bare,
save for a few yellow leaves stubbornly
hanging from tips heavy with snow. One
falls, flutters and my eyes follow like it's
a dying butterfly. I pick it up, hold it to
my nose and inhale all the universe's
intentions.   I step off the rock and
return to where I left, but Ryan's not on
the steps anymore. Toto and I walk onto the
porch, and I brush snow from Ryan's chair
then knock on the sliding door.

"Come in."

I go in, but Toto stays and eats snow.

"Up here, in my room."

The stairs are wide; the banister
shines. Each step has a give but doesn't
creak. Once at the top, I look down to the
front door, then go to his bedroom at the
end of the hallway.

Ryan holds up the painting he's
finished.

"It's beautiful."

I wince, wrap my arms around my stomach
and groan while falling onto the bed and
curling into a ball. Ryan stands over me;
then he's close. Now he's lying on his side

next to me. He speaks, but it's only vibration.

"Come lay with me," I say, as I tug him down to the bed, placing his hand below my ribcage and closing my eyes.

By the time my eyes open, the sun has begun to dip behind Apple Ridge. The light bending above the summit floats into his bedroom. We watch dust in front of the window swirl and spiral whenever a gust of wind blows.

"Let's get Flower tonight," I say.

"Tonight?"

"Yes."

"We're really doing this? Are you feeling up to it?" he asks.

"Oh! Damnit," I say.

He feels my liver jump. I know this because he massages my stomach.

"Let's go."

"Right now? We can't go. Something's seriously wrong with you."

"Yes, something is."

"We need to go to the hospital," he says.

"Can we please just go get Flower?"

"Maybe you should lie down? You're looking all squiddly."

"I'm freezing."

"You're sweating."

136

I throw my feet over the bed and stand up. My legs wobble; my knees totter. My brain evaporates into a thunderhead.

45
Ryan

The ambulance brought us to the cluster fuck that is Eastern Maine Medical Center. The Emergency Room was, and is, empty. Sylvia sits next to me and reads a big ass book she brought from home. Flat screen televisions live in every corner of this concrete waiting room; each shows a different station, and all are muted. I stare into one of the corners and close my eyes.

Sylvia nudges me around midnight, and a nurse takes us into an antiseptic hell. For now, Claire gets her own room with a view of a quick river lit all night by the casino. She puts a plastic cup of ice to her mouth and searches with her tongue for the finest of all crushed pieces. She snags one and hits a blue button, which turns on the machine pumping something into her veins. I close the curtains to block the city lights.

"Don't tell the doctor I found this."

Morphine.

Before Claire and I went to Pickering Square in Bangor, I would've bet my nuts that I'd swipe the needle from her and slip it in my vein. I would have waited until she was asleep, or I may have just asked, which she would have given it to me, but I don't care now. I look at the needle in her arm, the button that kicks on a pump that gives her fake opium, and that's cool. She can have it. I want none; I can finally paint again.

The nurse comes in. She's smiling, happy, obviously much too new, much too young.

"When can she go home?" asks Sylvia.

The nurse's pink smile fades.

"The doctor would just like to keep her until early tomorrow," she says, turning to a smiling Claire. "Then you should be able to go home."

Claire folds her hands together and lays them on her stomach, above the thin, white sheet.

"You can sleep now, Mom. It's almost one in the morning."

"I won't be able to. I'll just watch tv."

"Come lay with me, Ryan," says Claire as she turns on the television. "Check this out."

She turns the channel to a twenty-four hour marathon of Party of Five. "Pretty nice, huh?" We watch in silence for hours then Claire falls asleep, and I follow her.

I've been awake for half an hour, just long enough to get lost on the way to the cafeteria, to find it, buy a handful of whoopie pies, three large coffees and make it back just as Claire wakes and stretches in a room flooded with new sunlight.

"Coffees, my dears," I say, seeing Claire but no Sylvia. "Where's your mom?

"She's bringing the car around."

The nurse leaves, and Claire makes her bed. The Johnny spreads, and her butt pops out. I sneak up and pull her gown shut. She jumps.

"Oh. It's you," she says. "I thought the nurse came back."

"I guess you're feeling better," I say.

139

"You're one to talk about feeling, handsome."

"I never miss an opportunity."

She looks around the room, maybe at the shitty greeting card photos framed on the wall, or the plastic flowers on the window sill, or at the metal-framed bed with white sheets. She unties the gown, slides it off her arms and throws it to me.

"Turn around, please," she says while grabbing a pair of jeans and a maroon t-shirt from the end of the bed and gets dressed. She tugs on my elbow. "Come on. We have to get Flower."

I squeeze Claire's hand and follow her to the car, get in the back, and we head for home. Sylvia parks at the end of Ruby Lane, and we get out of the car.

The morning is not warm, and it's not cold. My hoodie's not too much, Sylvia's long sleeved L.L. Bean thing works, and Claire's t-shirt isn't too little. A gust blows a long brown curl onto Claire's lips, and she pulls it out with a single finger, allowing the breeze to lay it behind her ear.

"Ready?" Sylvia asks while we look across at the Ocean Side farm.

The wind dies, Route 1 is empty, and the grunts and goings-on of piggies crawl in like the songs of peeping frogs.

"Let's go," Claire says.

"Right now?" I say. "In the daylight?"

We cross the road into the Ocean Side parking lot, duck below a row of freshly-cleaned work trucks, and creep behind the barns until we get to the end.

46
Claire

Ryan walks behind me; surely, he's staring at my butt again. I laugh, and he doesn't ask why. There are Ocean Side pickups, but no farmhands, no drunk hicks, no murderous, evil bastards. There are only aluminum buildings, lined up and disappearing into a hilly field that eventually plummets into the harbor. We walk down the slushy road, trying to stay within the tire tracks, and listen to the hollow chimes of caged animals as we pass each barn.

"Is that a pond?" I ask.

"You smell that, Claire?" asks Ryan. "That's the shit pit. That's where all the piggy poo gets pumped to."

141

"It's almost pretty with the deep ring of snow around it," says Mom.

"A beautiful, chocolate lake," says Ryan.

"Gross."

"What? As long as we're wishing…," he says and opens the door to the last barn. The smell suffocates me. It's way worse in here today. The place has got to be almost a hundred degrees. The pigs, covered in sores, stand in their feces that's matted to the floor grates.

I cry as we walk within the hollow clanging of metal cage rails. The dust and dander are everywhere, and it thickens my tears like flour does broth. As we walk down the aisles, the swine speak in waves of grunts, these queer, tiny sounds, like happy popcorn popping, but once we've walked passed their cages and hope is gone, they return to gnawing on the metal rails just as those in front of us begin their happy popping.

We round the corner, and number eighty-two is empty.

"We're too late," I say.

"Either they killed her, or she's finally free," Mom says.

"Maybe both," I add.

"Thanksgiving is only a month away," she replies, pretending not to hear me.

Ryan walks to the empty cage and swings the gate back and forth.

"Hopefully, we can find her before they do," he says as we stare into an empty gestation crate unsuitable for a guinea pig. We walk out the back door after searching the aisles for a stray pig, but she is nowhere.

"Let's go this way. I want to check out the poo pond," he says.

"Why?" I ask, but he only shrugs and starts walking. Mom and I glance at each other, then follow him down a plowed road snaking through a snowy pasture.

"I'm turning around," I tell him.

"Me too," agrees Mom. "This smells way too bad."

"Okay, but we may have to wait for them," he says while pointing a finger at the truck a few hundred feet away that's coming toward us.

We look for a place to hide, but there's nothing out here except a stand of trees beside the sea of shit. Having no other choice than to face these people again, we sneak off and lay in the snow.

"I'll turn the pump on," someone says.

"There was a guy at the last farm I worked at in Montana that fell into one of these things."

"Shitty way to die," says the other.

"Sure is."

"I almost fell in once, but stopped before it went over my waist."

"You probably loved it, didn't you, Bobby?"

"I wasn't too afraid. A fat bastard like me will float just fine," he says with a laugh.

"I'd like to push them in," I whisper to Ryan, and he nods.

"I might be taking the plunge soon."

"Feel like going for a swim, Bobby?"

"The wife won't get off my case about money. I'd do anything not to have to hear that again. 'Give me money. Kids need cleats for soccer, shorts for basketball'. I told her I'm not raking blueberries again. I'm too old for that. She can go sell herself in Brewer if she wants more." Somewhere a motor turns on. "Just my luck, there'll be a big goddamn air pocket waiting for me down there, enough to keep me living for a while."

"Maybe you'll get that promotion."

"If we ever get that goddamn land, maybe."

"Stop complaining. Get in," says the pump man.

Two doors shut and they're gone.

"Let's go," I say.

We stand, brush off the sticky snow and walk in the tire's muddy tracks to the last barn, where we go around back and follow our trail to the parking lot.

Mom drives slowly up Ruby Lane. Orioles and blue jays flit back and forth. Ryan spots a cardinal, but he calls it a "real beautiful mother[effer]".

We go past his house, as if it's a natural move not to drop him off, and continue to ours.

We get out of the car, and Ryan runs to the door to let out Toto.

"I can't believe Flower's gone," I say and take the collar of my shirt and wipe my eyes. "I feel dirty. I need to take a bath." I walk to the door and turn around. "Ryan, have a seat. You can tell Mom all about how you saw me naked today."

I stop by the bedroom and take two pills then go into the bathroom, get undressed and turn the water on as hot as it will go without melting my flesh. I open the window above the tub and get goosebumps as the incoming cold air weaves with the warm already around me. The gust blows the hair

145

from behind my ear, but then it quiets and what's left is a soft whistle of wind coming down from the top of Apple Ridge.

"Ouch. Damn," I say while stepping into the boiling cauldron.   I hold my breath and slide down until my butt hits the bottom, then I lean back, feeling the sweat popping out of my flesh and beading on every pore above the waterline.

Downstairs, the front door opens then shuts. Ryan and Mom are talking as the house begins to smell like sweet marijuana. I lay back as the water cools to room temperature and watch my belly button pulse with the beating of my heart.

The air blooms with the scent of baking apple pie, or maybe it's pumpkin. I drain the hot water then fill the tub with cold. My breathing becomes shallow as the ice water climbs my body. Within a moment, I am acclimated, and there is equilibrium again, as if there wasn't before.

Maybe I'll get hypothermia. If my body gets to ninety, I'll be dead, but soon enough, I'll be thirty-three degrees for days on end, in a month, a week, a day; I haven't yet decided.

I stand up, let the water drip away, then dry off, put on pajama bottoms and a tank top then go downstairs. The warmth from

146

the baking oven presses into me like a heavy blanket on a cold night. Mom and Ryan sit at the table by the window, playing cards and talking like they're old friends. They each pull out a chair for me.

"Don't make me decide. I love you both."

"Are you high?" asks Mom.

My body is light, my heart warm.

"Yes. Yes, I am."

"Come on Professor, you used to be such a good girl," says Mom. "She's a hot teacher, huh? Could you imagine being in her class, listening to the brilliance coming from this hottie?"

Ryan blushes and lays down his hand. I consider the two empty seats again and sit next to Mom.

"Come on," he says, with his long, tattooed arms spread out.

"I gave birth to her, honey. Don't take it to heart."

"Is that rain?" I ask.

"It's pouring," Mom answers.

Toto barks.

I bend down and pick him up, holding his cute little face an inch from mine. I cradle him in my arms, and he stays there, looking up and nervously licking his black lips before I set him down. He runs to the door and scratches it, whimpering and growling. I go to the oven and open the door to smell the baking pumpkin pie.

"Nope. Let it go," she says. "Don't you open it anymore."

She runs over and slaps my hands away. "You can't take it out too early; it'll ruin it."

"Then I shall close the door," I say.

She puts my face in her hands and squeezes them together. Toto barks. Ryan gets up, goes to him and pets his head.

"What's the matter Lassie?" he asks. "You want to go out?"

He opens the door, and a blast of cold air shoots into the house like an angry spirit.

"You've got to see this," he says to us.

We go over and squeeze in front of him. Long strings of silver rain fall beyond the porch roof, and there, three feet in front of the steps, is a beautiful, pregnant Flower looking up at us and snorting as the rain cleans her.

Ryan

47

There she is, a big, fat pig playing in the new rain while her hooves are in the snow.

"She's the size of a chest freezer," says Claire.

Lightning whips the top of Apple Ridge as Sylvia lights a bowl. We creep forward until the rain falls only a foot away from the tips of our noses and pass the pipe around, quietly watching the rain patter on this gigantic animal and the drenched mutt next to her.

"Do you think she's ever seen rain before?" Claire asks.

"Doubt it," I say.

Flower trots around, inquisitive, then frantic. She buries her snout in a snow bank.

"Let's bring her down to your barn," Claire says. "Oh, I'm so happy you found us, Flower."

"We should go while it's not raining so hard," says Sylvia.

Claire bends down and rubs Flower's neck.

"Let's go, sweetie."

We're in the barn in five minutes, and we're soaked.

"There's the stable right," I say as we make it halfway down the dirt-floored barn.

Claire walks in and coaxes Flower, but once we're there, Flower sticks her nose up at the wooden gate.

"I guess we can't lock you up. You didn't travel this far for that," she says.

"Claire, I'm going to get a change of clothes for us before we die of pneumonia," Sylvia says.

As Sylvia leaves, Claire and I stand in front of one another; rain still slowly dripping from our fingertips, our soaked shirts suck at our bodies. We pause without thought to look at each bump and curve, every perfection and imperfection. I try to speak, but the words trip on my lips.

"I'm going to get a change of clothes," I finally say.

"See you in a bit, then, Mr. Alexander."

48
Ryan

I turn around and see Claire through the rain, backlit in the barn door, her bare feet kissing the slush with each step. When she gets to me, I turn over my palms to catch rain and move my shadow so the barn light shows the blue rain sliding down her face.

Our lips shake, but when they touch they are neither warm or cold, dry, or wet. I didn't know it a minute ago, but the stardust made our lips so that when they press like a tired head onto a pillow, somewhere, wind passes over a sand castle. Our bodies shiver, teeth chatter, lips quiver, but there is warmth where our bodies meet, and so we touch.

Claire

Silver rain drops drop;
  Bellied clouds zip by ears, thump
  Shoulders and shake earth.
The clear veil is granite,
  Yet we move through fluid
  Like we are fluid.

50
Claire
     The rain's lessened so that I can pick
out each bulbous drop as it hits my
shoulders. I snatch his wet, slippery hand
while we walk to his back porch and sit
under the roof, listening to a heavy rain
fade from a drum roll to only brushes on a
xylophone.
     "There's a falling star," he says as
the clouds part to a black sky.

"Right through Orion's belt."

"That must hurt the old guy."

The rain still falls out there, in the darkness. It falls from the tips of spruce and pine needles, and when I close my eyes, the storm was not a storm at all, but a vanishing pathway to its calm center.

"The doctor said I'll be dead before New Years," I say.

"What a dick."

I haven't cried yet, but I do now. It mixes with laughter and, even though it sounds happy, it is equally sad.

"I wouldn't trust him. He's probably telling a kid right now drugs and cigarettes are bad."

"The fire's hot inside, my dear. Come on in and dry off until your mother gets back," he says, and we go inside.

I stand near the couch and watch the firelight climbing the knots on the pine walls. Ryan runs upstairs, comes back, hands me a towel and sets a blanket in front of the fire.

"I'll put some more wood on," he says and throws on two logs.

"Are you done burning all your possessions?" I ask.

"What?"

"That pile that used to be there, books and photos, and stuff, are you done burning it?"

"We are now done being warmed by my former life."

"Wow."

"Deep, I know," he says.

I take my wet sweater off and warn him that it means nothing, that I'm going get dry then wrap up in the blanket. He nods.

Off come my wet clothes. I hang them by fire and sit on the floor with the blanket around my shoulders. Ryan joins me, leaning on his side, resting on an elbow. He looks up at me, and I kiss him as Mom comes in.

"I've been searching for you two birds," she says. "Flower's sleeping."

Then she sees us, takes in everything.

"I didn't mean to interrupt."

A smile comes on her face, one of those that couldn't be tamed at a funeral.

Mom leaves the clothes she brought for me on the counter and goes out to the barn.

Ryan stands up then helps me, and I get my dry clothes.

"Turn around, you," I say.

My reflection's in the kitchen window, as are his eyes while I pull an orange sweater over my head. Mom tells me it makes the purple flecks in my eyes shimmer, which is probably the reason she brought it down, to whore me out.

"We should get going," I say. He follows me out onto the porch. The sky has cleared, and I look up to Pegasus, where the Andromeda Galaxy spins. "Venus is supposed to be out sometime this month."

"I'd love to see her with you."

"Me, too."

"They ain't stars like this in San Francisco," he says.

"There ain't?" I ask.

"Nope. Ain't nothing of the sort."

I chuckle, or giggle, or maybe it's a laugh. Maybe they're different; maybe they're not.

The flood light on the barn lights up the wet world in front of us. The gravel shines, as does the grass poking out through the snow. Certain colors are made sharper: The red barn, the green shutters on the house, the stark white clapboards.

We continue toward the barn. Toto runs in and out of the door. He puts the brakes on, opens his mouth, looks at us, pants, growls, then runs back inside.

Ryan and I pause at the door to kiss, then, just as our lips begin to swell, headlights invade Ruby Lane, and a vehicle pulls into Ryan's. The man gets out and walks to us then stops in a circle of generated light.

Ryan turns his head so the tendon going up the side of his neck stands solid as a pier.

"I have no idea," he says.

"Seen my pig?" calls the stranger.

"Nope," Mom says.

"You sure?"

"Yep."

"You want to sell us the property yet?"

"Nope."

"Okay, then. Holler if you find the pig. I've got a great new marinade. We'll be seeing you," he says, hitches up his pants and walks away.

51
Ryan

We slept in the barn last night and woke up to a goddamn truck horn. That was about thirty seconds ago. There's nothing more irritating than waking to a truck horn. I go out and up comes this oafish douche bag all like "where's my fackin pig? Where's she?"

I want to run so I don't rip his face off. I'm no good at this stuff. He's coming up with a tire iron but doesn't make eye contact.

"You don't want to lose that bet, huh, Cheerio Von Peepers?" I say.

"Put that away, big guy," Sylvia says.

"Look, I just don't want any trouble from this guy," he says, pointing the tire iron at me.

"She's the mean one," I say and nod to Claire.

"Shut it," she says.

"Why are you so afraid of him?" Sylvia asks.

"I know you aren't from here, but this guy's crazier than pig shit. The bastard killed his own father, maybe the mother, too."

I step forward.

"Hold on," he says, pointing the tire iron.

"Oh?"

"That's what everyone's saying. You killed them."

"So why'd you risk your life to come up here for one little pig?" I ask.

"Because she's mine and I'm not going to let anyone take what's mine," he says.

"Well, Chum, I guess on that we agree."

"Just let me have her back and I won't call the police," he says.

"Why do you think she's here?" asks Claire. "We told the guy last night we didn't have her."

"Some of the boys said they saw three people matching your description running through the field the other night, two nice pieces and a tall bastard. You took her before, why not again? Besides, I hear some of my men roughed up this guy."

Claire walks up to him.

"Just go back to work. Leave us be," she says.

"I am working, just finished my first coffee break."

I step next to Claire.

"Just get outta here, see?" I say and take a step forward so I can smell the coffee on his breath.

He raises the tire iron.

"Back up, son," he says.

"Daddy?"

52
Claire

Ryan's calm, like all emotion is lost.
I never thought someone could appear so sure
of themselves, so together in such an
intense situation. In the short time I've
known him, I've never seen Ryan this
relaxed. I press my shoulder onto his arm so
he knows he's not alone.

"Just give me the pig and I'll be out
of here."

"No," he says, "and put that thing
away. You ain't gonna swing that club,
Daddy. Yah ain't got it in ya."

There is a drugged sweetness, a lustful
joviality in Ryan's eyes that betrays the
violent situation. I should be more worked
up than I am, but Flower's safe, Mom's safe.
I'm on an extended painkiller ride; Heaven's
mana.

"Now that I'm up here where the light's
shining real good on you, those stories
can't be true. You ain't shit," he says to
Ryan.

Ryan swings. Hits. The man collapses.

"Are you okay?" says Mom to the man
still dreaming with his eyes open.

"She's mine. Not yours. This isn't right," he says.

Ryan steps back after the punch and looks at the man on the ground.

"You need to leave," I say.

He grumbles and moans, stumbles, falls, gets up, speaks.

"Where's the fucking pig?" he asks as he wipes the blood off his chin, smearing it across his jaw and wrist.

"Forget about Flower," I say.

He gathers his balance, standing completely still, then stumbles across the lawn, gets in his truck and drives down Ruby Lane.

In an odd way, we're elated. How's a person supposed to act when they're one of three, or at least two pacifists who just won a fist fight? We feel the warmth, the fear, the trembling and joy within us. We stew in bubbling animosity, saying little things my memory cannot find space for, but my heart finds titillating.

Once our blood pressures lower, Ryan goes inside his house for some blankets and to call a vet while Mom and I go to the barn and find Flower still asleep with a cowering, shivering Toto behind her; he doesn't like violence.

53
Ryan

It's hours past midnight and chilly as hell, but the blankets make it pretty nice. I'm the only one awake and should be able to sleep, but my eyes won't shut off, no matter how comfortable this straw bed is.

Twenty feet up, a black mouse runs along the rafters, knocking off dust and pebbles on his way. The whole time I grew up here, I never came out to the barn, laid down, and looked up. It's a cathedral in here, a cathedral fit for five hobos. Sylvia and I smoked a bowl an hour ago, and she hasn't moved since, so I have these holy halls all to myself. Flower's snoring like a happy grandfather. Claire's nose whistles, but it's cute, seriously cute. I brush her lip with the tip of my finger, just enough so she doesn't wake up, but so it tickles both of us, then I lay back, close my eyes, and finally sleep.

I don't know how much later, but I open my eyes and watch the barn slowly brighten. There's a blond light coming through the cracks that turns Claire's hair the same color. She probably feels me staring because she stirs and sits up while rubbing her eyes. Sylvia leaps over to Flower.

"A piglet!" she cries. "Another! She had her babies last night."

Flower rolls around then lays her head back down, resting for only a second, though, before she's cleaning her piglets and showing them the way to the snack bar. We watch them until the sun rises high enough to declare officially that morning has arrived.

"I'm going to make coffee. You ladies want anything?" I ask.

"Coffee," says Sylvia.

"Pancakes," says Claire.

"I don't think I have stuff for pancakes," I cautiously confess.

Claire lets out a melodramatic "huff".

"Fine. I guess I'll just starve," she says.

"Wait, honey," says Sylvia. "We have some mix up at the house."

"I'm on it," I say.

"You don't have to go. You make coffee. I'll get the mix," says Claire.

Sylvia speaks up, "Toto and I'll watch the little guys."

"Come on," says Claire, as she grabs my elbow and hauls me out.

"I want a full cup of coffee as soon as it's ready!" shouts Sylvia.

Claire and I walk together and, before she goes her way and I go mine, I see her as I had when she was naked in the living room: soaked, peaceful as a junky sitting by the fire.

"Get the oven hot," she calls. "I'll be back in a minute to show you how to cook the best breakfast."

I turn to the house when I hear a vehicle driving up Ruby Lane. A busted Ocean Side truck pulls into my driveway, and a guy waddles toward me.

These Ocean Side shits wear the same uniform: shit covered clothes, shit covered teeth, shit covered hat hiding shit-greased hair. This guy has one more thing than he did last night, though, a revolver on his belt.

"Those are some fine accouterments," I say.

If Claire was here, I'd be listening to the prettiest laughter in the world. Instead, I get to hear this guy cough up chocolate-mayonnaise-phlegm.

"What do you want?" I ask.

"I want my fucking sow back. She's due any day."

"We don't have her," I say.

"I know you've got her. You can give her up, or I can get her."

He pets the revolver.

"How's the chin? Are those stitches or whiskers?"

"Where is she?"

"Look," I say, "we have her, but you're not getting her."

I take a step forward. He flips the button on the holster, takes out the gun and points it at the ground.

"Where is she?"

"Get out of here. You're not doing shit," I say.

"Yeah?"

"Why are you doing this all over a pig?"

He steps to me.

"Why aren't you selling us this land?"

"Why do you care?"

"I was going to run the whole thing, worked my whole life for it."

"Are you a prostitute Peeps Q?"

"No," he says. "You're not keeping the fucking pig, either."

I reach for the gun and then the butt crashes down on my head. Dead, wet grass pokes the inside of my nose as gravel in the slush rakes my jaw. My vision blurs. My eyes close, maybe sleep, then they open when a gun's fired. Two more ring out. Toto yips and sprints out of the barn. Sylvia screams.

"Where's Mom? Are you okay?" asks Claire.

She leans over me, out of breath, with a box of pancake mix in her shaking hand.

"Wait here. Please, Claire." I try to get up but fall back onto warm, red snow. "Don't go in there," I beg, but she's already through the barn door. "Claire! Wait!"

54
Claire

"Claire! Don't!" Mom screams.

"I hope you die a miserable death," I say to the vicious bastard as he puts the gun back into the holster. "What about

Flower? You asshole. What are we supposed to do?"

My eyes close, and I breathe slowly, focusing on the way my shirt pulls on my chest as I inhale and then how it relaxes, softening like a fleece blanket. Tears forge an icy creek as they trail down my cheek.

I open my eyes and pound the chest protecting his dead heart, attempting to break through and squeeze life back into it. I slap his face, but he smiles and bats me away.

"Never touch my daughter. I'll kill you!"

"No, you won't," he says and walks out.

Mom stands next to Flower, whose blank eyes line up with a horseshoe tacked to the opposite wall. I kneel and run my fingers over her wounds dripping with blood thick as maple syrup.

Two piglets lay just below her swollen nipples. Toto licks their faces and tries to wake them with nudges from his wet nose.

"So young," Mom says while swallowing thick tears.

Toto goes to Flower and licks the blood from her belly, then trots behind her and digs in the straw. He growls, yips, then licks the giant pink nose of a small-headed

piglet who chose to sleep on its mother's
backside last night.

"She's alive," says Mom.

"I don't believe it."

"Where's Ryan? He needs to see this."

"I don't know, Mom. Be right back."

I go outside, and he's not on the
ground. I walk to the back porch, slide the
door open.

"Ryan? Are you here? Hello?"

I walk around to the front of the house
and look out over the treetops that tumble
down for a mile to the ocean. A scream
carries up from Ruby Lane and echoes off
Apple Ridge.

"Ryan!" I call, and when he doesn't
respond, I go toward the scream.

I run off his lawn and down Ruby Lane
and with each step, the impact shoots
through my body. It becomes difficult to
breathe, hard to let air out, which is
somehow worse than not being able to let it
in.

Around the corner, I see the Ocean Side
truck, and as I crest the hill, I see them
off to the side, under an apple tree. Ryan's
knelt beside him, or what's left of him.
Ryan wipes the sweat and blood from his
face, looms over the caved-in, broken,
sludgy mess before him and sets the man's

tire iron onto a tree trunk that's still wet from the rain.

I am a ghost, and nobody sees me; I place both hands on a tree, rest the corner of my mouth on the cold bark, peek around and watch Ryan pick up the man and put him in the bed of the truck. Ryan closes the tailgate and gets in. The engine starts, and I watch them rolling forward until they turn a corner and disappear down the mountain. I can't help but believe, with a dash of jealousy, the dead man won the fight, and this gives me an idea.

I walk up Ruby Lane, oddly, in no hurry. I stop to watch a gray squirrel pick apart spruce cones, then again to listen to a chickadee sing it's name. I even watch the only maple leaf left on a giant tree. I wait for it to fall, but it never does. I loiter on Ryan's front lawn where the tire hangs, get in and swing in wide circles while icy water from inside the ring splashes on my butt. I get out and walk to the barn. Toto meets me outside and follows me to Mom.

"We need to get her some food, honey," Mom says.

"What do we feed her?"

"Milk, I guess. What's the matter?" she asks.

"Nothing. Why?"

168

"You're pale. You should lie down."

"I'm fine. I'll go see if Ryan has any milk."

I walk to Ryan's, go in the back door and get the carton of milk from the refrigerator and wonder why more people don't drink it right off the teet.

I grab a bowl then wonder how a piglet's going to drink out of it. I shuffle around the cupboards and drawers then begin assembling a baby bottle using a styrofoam cup, an elastic, and a sandwich baggie. I finish putting it together on the way out.

"Nice, MacGyvering," says Mom as I hand her the contraption.

"Mom, Ryan didn't get a chance to call the vet today. I'm going to go call them. Do you need anything else before I go?"

"No, Sweetie. I'm okay. Everything'll be fine."

She passes me her phone, and as I leave, I stop outside the door to smell the sunshine drying the grass as Mom sings a lullaby she once sung to me.

55
Sylvia

I'm laying on the straw and high on the weed, experiencing what a psychiatrist might call "numbing". I sing Standing on the Moon to the piglet as her massacred family lay behind us.

When she grows up, every time she looks out through grayed fence posts, at grasshoppers perched on the tips of golden rod, at Claire's chickens as they purr and pick ticks from between the hoppers and the dandelions, she'll see a thriving, teeming universe that didn't allow her a mother, a brother, a sister.

I'm petting Pollen; that's what I named her. I turn and Ryan's walking up to me, throwing each foot in front of the other like he's dragging concrete blocks. His shirt's torn at the collar. A sheet of brown blood has dried on his face. Ryan's eyes, which are normally clear, attractive, intuitive, are blank, zen. He stops a few feet from me, next to Flower's head, and I

170

watch his eyes move as they study the bloody
mess surrounding us.

"Ryan, why are you bleeding?" I grab
his hand and look closer.

"Let's go to the doctor. Come on," I
urge.

"It's fine," he says as he pulls it
back. "I killed a man for harming us."

"Like Moses?" I ask.

He laughs.

My numbness fades and interest and
anger grows in me like a bomb.

"Why are you telling me this?"

He looks at Flower then tugs at a tear
in his shirt.

"I had no choice."

"Ryan, what did you do?"

"He won't be shooting that gun again,"
he says.

"Did he attack you?"

He sits next to me. I hold the pig like
a baby and stand up, rocking her in my arms.
"Ryan, was it self-defense?"

"It was defensive."

He sticks out a bloody hand to pet
Pollen. I pull her close and run out of the
barn.

"Wait."

Ryan rushes out, puts his hand on my
shoulder and turns me around.

"I'll turn myself in," he says, as the clouds begin to shower. "Please let me wait until Claire's gone."

"Ryan. Please, stop."

"I'm sorry," he says and wraps his arms around me. "I didn't mean anything by it. Please stop crying."

I step back, wipe my eyes, grab his forearm and feel the scabbed needle holes.

"I know nothing about what happened, okay? Just promise to do whatever Claire wants. Keep her happy."

"I promise."

"Anything she asks."

"Anything at all."

"Good."

"I threw him in the shit pit and ran his truck in," he says.

"I don't want to know. You need to change your clothes before Claire sees you."

56
Ryan

Claire and Sylvia left with Pollen to go to the vet. That was a few hours ago, and I'm here, on the porch of the house I gave to Sylvia. It's twilight, and I'm covered in mud and filth from burying the pigs.

I stretch out my legs, sit way back in the chair and wait for a murder of crows to fly over the space between Claire's house and mine.

I can't sit still, and I can't do anything since the rain has really started coming down, cats and dogs, some might say. If only they were lemon drops and gumdrops. I toss my cigarette out on the wet lawn, take my clothes off, and run like hell through the field. The rain's so thick it's like I'm hidden in fog.

The water's warm, the evening cold. I scrape the mud and blood from my body then fall to the earth and roll around, jump up and let the rain and wind take everything away.

I run inside, grab a towel, dry off, change my clothes then run back out onto the porch and rock in a chair not meant to be rocked, teetering and tottering while rain pounds the ground. Black rivers and streams weave down the hill from Claire's, making a dark pond or two on the journey down.

I can hardly see her house way up there behind all this rain. It's just a couple of blurry boxes in a gray world. It's strange to think that when I was back in California,

Claire and I looked up at the same moon, the same sun. If I knew where Venus was, we could have seen her, too. Maybe we'll find Venus together.

Inside, the house phone rings. I let it go to the answering machine.

"Hello? Ryan? Please, pickup. Hello?" I go inside and get it.

"Hi, Nicole. Are you drunk?"

Silence, then a lighter flicks.

"Drunk? Am I drunk? Are you drunk?"

"Why are you calling?"

"I just missed you. That's all. I watched the weather, and you're supposed to be getting a big snow storm," she says.

"I haven't heard anything about that. It's raining now."

"Two feet of snow. How haven't you heard about it?" she asks.

"I guess I've just been busy," I say.

"Did you sell the property?"

"Nope, but one of the goons came up to talk about it."

"So, are you never coming back to California?"

"I don't know. Maybe. I may go find a nameless stream and become a nameless thing."

"Ryan, you know how I said we were shooting the film in Massachusetts?"

"kinda."

"Well, I got them to change the location to Maine."

"Okay. You need to promise me that if you come over, you'll treat Claire and Sylvia like friends."

"That's another part of the reason I'm calling. I was thinking, If we can't be together, I still want to be friends. I just got jealous. That's all. I'm sorry."

"Give me a call when you get in," I say.

"That's another part of the reason I'm calling," she says as
I look out the living room window and see headlights floundering in the foggy, damp night.

57
Claire

"Pollen will love it here," Mom says as we walk toward a single barn set on one hundred acres of hilly pasture.

"It is beautiful."

"Glad to hear it," says the farmer.

"Especially since the rain stopped for a minute," I say as I step barefoot into a puddle.

"Let's go meet your new mommy," Mom says to Pollen, who's curled in her arms.

"Toto come back here!" I call.

He stops, turns around, then sprints to me.

"I know it's your decision, but it's fine with me if he wants to run around," says the farmer the veterinarian sent us to.

"Thank you. Go, run. Have fun, Toto."

He bends down to look in Pollen's eyes, smiles and tickles her chin.

"I'm glad Dr. Andrews told you to come here," he says.

"What's your name?" I ask.

"Ron."

"Nice to meet you, Ron."

Mom smiles and nods at him.

"Hello," she says.

"Howdy. Beatrice is right up here."

He stops and takes a cigar from a purple package I've seen behind convenience store counters, lights it and says, "but we call her Betty."

"I love it," I say.

The barn is the size of a grade school gymnasium. The siding is gray from years of enlisted protection, but the window frames are freshly white.

"Here, bring her around this way. Watch your step," he says, as three white hens cross in front of us to avoid a puddle. Ron opens the door to Betty's pen. "She usually has the run of the property, but it's just safer in here while she's nursing, especially with all the rain."

"It's the size of a living room," Mom says.

"We try to keep her happy."

Mom lifts Pollen to her face, rubs noses and walks into Betty's tranquil bedroom.

"I suppose this is goodbye, little baby," she says.

I rub down the fragile bumps of Pollen's spine, and Mom sets her in front of Betty. Pollen wiggles and wrestles her way into the pile of hungry siblings.

"They're a glob of night crawlers," I say.

This makes Ron laugh as he blows out smoke that smells like brown sugar.

"You can pick her up in a month if you want. She'll be weaned by then," says the sweet man.

"Thank you, Ron, but I'll have moved by then," I tell him. Mom grabs my wrist.

"What about you, dear? Are you moving too?" he asks Mom.

"Mr. Alexander, I'm Officer Smithe."

"Snow's coming, boss. You wanna come in?"

"Sure."

"You want to sit next to the fire?" I ask.

"I'll stand."

"What can I do for you?"

"An Employee with Ocean Side's Farm has disappeared, Bobby Lancing."

"Terrible, terrible news," I say.

"It is. He was a good friend. Anyway, they said he was coming up here to look for one of their pigs, something about selling the land, too. Did you see him that day?"

"Sure, he stopped by. He didn't find the pig, and I'm not selling, so he left."

"Did he say anything about where he might be going?"

"Nothing at all," I say.

"You sure?"

"Well, he did say something about being pissed about having to go do something at a shit pit."

"They never mentioned that. You're sure?"

"That I am, Pedro."

"The name's Dan," he says.

"Well, Dan, I've got some strapping down to do before the storm hits. Let me know if you need anything else."

"Since you're the last one to have seen him, I'll probably be in touch again," he says.

"That makes complete sense," I assure him.

"Oh, before I leave, I ran over a tire iron on the way up. I set it out on the porch so nobody gets a flat. I figure it's either yours or your neighbor's up there."

"Thank you very much. I'll be sure and take care of that," I say.

"Have a nice day," he says.

"Carry on, now."

59
Claire

I'm in my room, sitting cross-legged on
the bed, sometimes reading Ethan Frome,
other times being hypnotized by the rhythmic
falling of snow outside the window. Inside
is the smell of dinner in an antique house,
an Italian-scented heaven created by my very
own mother.

This makes me feel like a teenager in
our home back in Georgia. It's warm in here,
like fluffy warmth, warmth you hold and
cuddle. I'm reading over my student's papers
on Dylan Thomas that I honestly never
graded, but logged A's for each before
leaving my job, and it's got me thinking
about suicide.

Mom calls up, and her voice makes me
smile.

"Yes?" I say.

"Gilmore Girls starts in five. Come on.
We can have dessert before dinner!" she
says.

The thought of more sticky-sweet sugar
makes me ill. It's been a few days since
Ryan buried Flower, and in those days, I've
eaten enough coconut ice cream and molasses
cookies to satisfy any mourning pains.

I set the papers next to me and get out
of bed, pull a pair of neon green shorts up
my legs, a maroon tank top down my body, and
go see Mom in the living room.

She's on the couch with a plate of
lasagna on her lap and another on the coffee
table. I grab the plate from the table and
sit down beside her. The basket of garlic
bread is between us.

"What happened to dessert?" I ask.

"It was a nasty joke. We've been pity-
eating for too many days, sugar plum. No
more goddamned sugar."

"No more goddamned sugar," I say. Her
eyes widen as if a ten-year-old just cussed.
"What?"

"Nothing. I'm just not used to hearing
you talk like that, sailor."

Toto leaps off the couch and runs to
the front door, shooting his teeny shotgun-
barks all the way there. I go to the door
and open it to reveal a tall, darkly dressed
Ryan, backdropped by a blizzard.

"Come in. How did you even get up
here?"

"I left a while ago, stopped to rest twice to make snow angels then, somehow, eventually landed on the front door of a beautiful maiden."

"Stop," I say, blushing. "I can't even see your house through the snow."

He laughs as I shut the front door.

"Yeah, I got lost, but thankfully I could retrace my steps before the storm buried my tracks."

"Thank God for that."

He brushes the snow from his shoulders and the top of his head and starts wiping down at his waist.

I take his cold hands in mine.

"Come on. Gilmore Girls is about to start."

"I know. I hurried to get here in time," he says. "I've got to tell you something."

"Shoot."

"Nicole's coming to visit. I'm sorry. I made her promise not to be such a bitch."

"That's fine," I say.

"You're not upset?"

"There are few things that upset me, and having one of your friends visit is not one of them."

"I thought she was filming in Massachusetts, though?"

"I guess they needed this blizzard for a scene."

"It is beautiful."

"She wants to apologize, too."

"It's fine. Grab a plate of food and come in before we miss Gilmore Girls," I say and go into the living room.

He comes in with a full plate and sits next to me. My liver starts to hurt, and with that pain comes nausea. I just took a pill, but I hurry to my room, take two more, then take my seat between Ryan and Mom.

By the first commercial, the pain's slipping away, but I suppose, in the end, there's only one cure for suffering, and each day I come closer and closer to swallowing that pill. I put my hand on Mom's lap and my head on Ryan's shoulder.

I didn't take enough to overdose, but as the minutes roll on, and my eyelids slide down, I pray that being here, in this living room at the dead end of Ruby Lane, is the last feeling I ever have.

"Be right back," says Mom. "Now that you two are here, I've got a surprise."

"Exciting!"

"Are you going to eat?" Ryan asks as Mom leaves the living room.

"No. My stomach's upset," I say as I look to make sure Mom's left the room. I set my plate on the coffee table and pet my lap so Toto jumps. "Ryan, I want you to kill me."

"What the fuck are you talking about?"

"I saw you…"

"Saw me what?"

"...kill that man. I'm dying soon and the pain's beginning to make living unbearable. When the time comes, I want you to help. Mom can't see me rot like I saw Gram.

"I can't kill you."

"Consider it helping Mom, for me. You weren't bothered by doing what you did. You were happy."

"You don't understand," he says.

"Why?"

"I've never loved anyone other than you, and your mom made me promise to do anything you wanted."

"Anything?"

"Anything."

"Oh, the possibilities. I love you, Ryan Alexander," I say. "You're like a psychopath with a heart, a real cliche."

"A real handsome cliche'."

"Ryan, will you be honest with me?"

He takes a bite of garlic bread and a sip of orange soda.

"Go."

"What they say is true, isn't it? About your parents?"

He takes another drink of soda.

"Dad killed Mom."

"What about your father?"

"He killed me first."

"I don't blame you for anything. Just help me overdose. That's all, maybe hold my hand."

Mom walks back into the room with a wrinkled magazine.

"Look what I found while unpacking," she says and holds up a vintage copy of Highlights for Children then hands it to me. "It's the very first poem Claire ever published, and it's about you, her little boyfriend."

I flip the pages until I see the words I wrote twenty-two years ago, a form of which I've never quite forgotten.

"I told you I wrote this."

"I believed you. Will you read it to me?" he asks.

"I guess," I say, blushing, then stand up and turn around to face them. I look at Ryan's painting, the one I bought at the record shop that hangs above the couch and begin to read my poem to the boy in the painting.

"'To My New Friend, written by Claire Michelle Addison: age five, Savannah, Georgia.'" I lower the magazine and witness two eager faces. "Are you sure you're ready?"

"We couldn't be more ready."

"Okay." I raise the magazine to my chest. "'To my new friend, The only boy is you that didn't say "ewww" because my favorite shoe is no shoe at all. I wear them most every day, just bare, plain old feet. "What happens if you get cut?" you asked. Mom comes and takes away the hurt. When you fell, though, Mom wasn't near, but thankfully she taught me well. I kissed your knee. We walked for miles, then swung all day until you smiled.'"

"You're amazing," he says.

"I've got the greatest daughter in the world."

"I'm a dork," I correct and sit back down, squeezing between them, trying to hide my flushed face and goofy smile.

60

Ryan

Claire wakes up around midnight, and
I'm watching Kesha and her beautiful life.

"What happened to the Gilmore Girls,
and where's Mom?"

"She went to bed an hour ago. It's
almost midnight," I tell her.

"Oh," she says as she rubs her eyes and
sits up, looking let down.

"What's the matter?" I ask.

"Nothing," she says, and squeezes next
to me, looping her arm through mine.

"Yeah. I meant to wake you, but I got
sucked into this show. I was going to carry
you up when it was over."

Claire takes the remote from my lap and
turns off the television. She looks up at me
with sleepy eyes and a dopey, adorable
smile.

"If you want, you can carry me up now."

61

Ryan

I'd like to write it all down,
everything that happened last night. I would
love to have a video, not in a perv sort of

way, but the way a parent would want a video of their child's birth. Parents say all the time that seeing their child born changes their life, alters the way they see the world. Children are LSD for squares; that's the feeling I got last night, only Claire is LSD for a junked-out murderer.

If I tried to write it down, it would sound like a doting, disillusioned parent. It would sound inflated, though it wouldn't be. It would sound saccharine, which it would be, but in all the right flavors.

Afterward, when we were lying in bed, I asked her what she was thinking:

"About your painting of us and my poem of us. You?" she asks.

"I hear music."

"It's quiet," she says. "Just the wind blowing snow from the few remaining petioles."

"Petioles?" I ask.

"Petioles," she confirms.

"Not music like that."

"Then music like what?"

"I hear two songs together."

"Yeah?"

"Yeah," I say.

She rolls onto her side and drapes her thin arm across my chest.

"Which ones?" she asks.

"I've never heard them before," I
confess.

She turns over, lies on her back, and
we hold hands between our bodies.

"I want to sing a corny song," she
says.

"I want to listen to you sing a corny
song."

"Lying in my bed I hear the clock tick.
If you're lost...," she begins with perfect
pitch.

Our eyelids close as her singing
becomes whispers which flatten, deaden, then
pulse, sounding like a heartbeat. Only thing
is, it's just a sleeping breath, soft as
cotton.

62
Claire

The storm ended, and now three feet of
snow covers our world. Thankfully, it
stopped this morning, but it still took us
forever to drive to my doctor's appointment
in Bangor.

I'm in a hospital room with Mom waiting
for the doctor to come in and hopefully give

me stronger drugs. Ryan's out in the lobby talking to some old man who's waiting for his wife to finish chemo.

Lately, it's been too obvious to ignore that my health is dropping down a deep, black well. I feel dehydrated no matter how much water I drink. My stomach is swelling, even Mom can't deny it now. There's a bulge as if I'm a few weeks along on a non-seminal birth, carrying this cancerous fetus.

I'm laid down on the crunchy paper they spread out on the table, feeling like a child in this thin, white gown. Mom's next to me, sitting in the doctor's chair and going through the cupboards, taking out tongue depressors and latex gloves. I know she's looking for a stethoscope, the Hope Diamond of the hospital mines, she claims.

"You can only get one when a doctor's been complacent and left theirs behind. So, you find a stethoscope, you find a new doctor."

I asked her if she'd ever found one. She hadn't, still hasn't. Yet she formed a philosophy around this idea and cannot set it aside. I was hoping she'd find one today. Not only would it be nice to see her smile, but it would be a reason to just not be here.

In typical hospital architecture, there are no windows, just plaster, filtered air and bleached sinks. An hour ago, when we left the outside world for this dungeon, it was a beautiful, gray day, the kind photographers love.

Mom rolls over in the doctor's chair and rests her head on my knees.

"How're you doing, sweetie?"

I run my fingers through her fine, silver hair. Ryan would have laughed at that. He'd say something like, "Damn, you got some fine, silver hair. Fine as hell, girl." I'd laugh as I laugh now.

"What's funny?" she asks.

"A hypothetical Ryan," I explain as nausea pools, and the room pulses with powerful waves.

I move deep within my brain; I've fallen from the Titanic and look up through six-and-a-third leagues of black to fading, shivering lanterns.

Once I can no longer see the burning wicks, my eyes open to a different room. Mom and Ryan are to my left. She's holding my hand, and Ryan is holding hers. Mom's lips move, but the words are mush as I try to dig through this drugged daze.

"You're here with us now," she says.

Her tear falls onto my chin.

"What happened?" I ask as she rubs it
off with her thumb then squeezes my hand.

"The cancer's spread, honey. It's
everywhere."

"I know."

My eyes become mid-air water balloons.
Mom bends, lays her chest on mine and
presses her warm, wet cheek onto my warm,
wet cheek. Ryan squeezes my shin and looks
down the length of my body.
His eyes are more empathetic than I
remember, bluer than I remember. They're
glossed and red from crying, and this
somehow makes them more beautiful. Ryan
nudges Mom, and she reaches over, pulls one
of the doctor's machines closer to me, grabs
a button on a short wire and puts it into my
hand.

"Morphine drip," she says. "Just press
the blue button whenever there's pain."

"I know how this works. Just don't let
the nurse catch me."

I press the button. Then again. And
once more. My body calms and begins to float
above itself.

"Who's got the remote?" I ask.

Ryan searches, takes it off his chair
and passes it to me.

"The Price is Right is on," I say, and
Mom and Ryan fade deeper into the background

192

as the contestant's wheel tic-toc's near the dollar spot.

I press the beautiful blue button one more time and fight to stay awake for the final showcase in hopes of seeing somebody win a rusted truck or a trip to Brewer, Maine, but I cannot remain, and so I ride on my awareness as it dissolves into my body.

63
Ryan

I haven't been home from the hospital for long. Claire's resting at her place, so I'm sitting down, doing a little painting, watching the fireplace, getting ready to go see her in an hour, but that might be awkward because Nicole just showed up.

"Hey, Ryan," she says, drops her purse and runs over to me, leaving snow prints all along the floor.

"Hey, Nicki. I didn't think you'd make it today. The snow's crazy."

"Do you have time for dinner?" she asks.

"I was going up to Claire's."

"Perfect. I need to apologize to them."

"Yeah?"

"Yes."

"Cool," I say.

"What're you painting?"

I move the canvas so she can see.

"Wow. Where was she when you were in art school? You'd be famous by now. Was she really swimming?"

"There was a record high, sixty-four, I think. It's right up the mountain, and the crazy lady was in there."

"Is it far from here?" she asks.

"Not too far. The way down is longer."

"Why?"

"Who leaves heaven in a hurry?" I ask.

"Only the interesting ones," she says.

"True. Let's go to Claire's. She just got out of the hospital last night, so I'm making blueberry pancakes for her."

"Jesus Christ. When did you get domesticated?" she asks.

"Yesterday."

We walk to the kitchen and out the back onto the porch, then we enter the snow corridor that will take us to Claire's front porch.

"Did you shovel this?" she asks.

"I did. All in my lonesome," I say. "There was a T.V. marathon I couldn't miss."

We each light a cigarette and look up to the stars, watching as the smoke cloud disappears high above us.

"Why was she in the hospital?" Nicole asks as we start walking.

"Liver cancer."

"Oh, God. How bad?"

"She'll be dead within the month," I say.

"How old is she?"

"Twenty-seven."

64
Claire

I open my front door to find Ryan and Nicole with cold noses and cheeks.

"Hey, Ryan. Welcome back, Nicole," I say and step aside.

"Thanks for letting me in after being so miserable."

"Of course," I say, as she hangs her coat on the rack, and walks to Ryan, who's getting blueberries from the fridge.

"Is there anything I can do?" Nicole asks Mom.

"How do you feel about dicing peaches for dessert?"

"I'd love to.".

"So, what do you do for work?" Mom asks while handing her a knife.

"I'm a film producer."

"Interesting. Are you working on anything now?"

She's a great peach cutter.

"Just a romantic comedy set in Massachusetts," Nicole says.

"I still think it sounds lame as fuck," Ryan says.

"What do you do?" Nicole asks Mom.

"I just retired last month and moved here from Georgia to be with Claire."

"Why are you filming in Maine if the movie's in another state?" I ask.

All three heads turn to me, and she grins.

"There are fewer leaves on the trees and a lot of snow here," she says. "It's what the scene calls for, you know?"

"Makes sense," I say and sit at the kitchen table, grab the deck of cards and deal solitaire.

"So, there's a Supremes cover band playing Friday at an old building down the road. Anyone interested in going?" Nicole asks.

"That must be at the Grange," says Mom. "I'll go."

"Me, too," says Ryan, "but only if Claire goes. I want the last dance."

"Of course, I'll go, but I get the first."

"Deal."

"These peaches are making my hands sticky," Nicole says while walking away from the chopping block and rinsing her fingers in the sink.

I look down at the solitaire spread before me and pick up the cards.

"This game's no fun without anyone else," I complain.

"I'll play a game with you," Nicole offers as she sits down and notices the picture of Ryan and me I put on the kitchen table.

"Is that you two?" she asks.

"How'd you know?" I ask.

"It looks like the painting Ryan hung in our apartment at art school. 'Two Beautiful Children Swinging Through a Beautiful Day', he used to call it."

"I had no idea," I say as my cheeks warm.

"So adorable," Nicole says.

"I bought a print and hung it in the living room."

"You're lucky. They're rare. What do you want to play?" she asks.

"Anything you want."

"Go Fish," she says.

"Great choice," I say and deal out our hands.

The house fills with the sound of a waterfall as Mom pours the first pancake into a frying pan.

"Ouch!" she jumps back, shaking her hand. "Screw you grease."

"Do you have a queen?" I ask.

"Only if you count Ryan," she says. "Go fish."

I pick a queen from the top of the deck and lay down the pair. Nicole tucks her cards to her cleavage and leans in.

"You look so healthy, but Ryan says you're dying."

"I have my days," I say, lay my hand down and walk out of the kitchen.

"Claire, honey, where are you going? Try a bite of this pancake," she says.

"I'll be right back. I need to get something," I say, walking into the living room then upstairs to my bedroom.

It's quiet in here. I've always thought it was like a Puritan schoolhouse. The floor creaks when I step. When the sun warms the walls, it smells like Gram's perfume, delivering a flower no matter the season.

The walls are papered blue, and it curls along each seam to show the yellowed glue that's worked flawlessly for over a century, but now looks as if it should be tossed out with the peach pits.

There are two open windows behind my headboard. I don't care that's it's thirty degrees out, or that the wind throws tiny ice crystals into my cheeks. I have a love affair with breezes: the scents they carry, the eternal journey they've traveled, the divine feeling it brings to my body knowing that the same wind may have wrapped around Ryan and me when we met on the tire swing.

The breeze surging through these windows is cold, and sharply so. It smells like snow, which smells like distilled water and wind. It's the absence of scent that makes it so unique; it is the absolute base of all smells: nothing, purity. Occasionally, there's a hint of a Christmas tree, and I think of my summer vacation when Mom and I stayed with Gram for a week. There was a Folger's commercial that played every thirty minutes, which Ryan and I watched each time, and there's steam rising from the cup of a young man who's just returned home for Christmas, which is odd because it was

July, maybe it was prerecorded. We're lying on the floor, our feet in the air, our stomachs pressed against the slippery hardwood, the same hardwood floor I just walked on. We're nervously existing together while watching Looney Tunes, though I'm secretly waiting for the coffee commercial again.

That breeze that came in just a moment ago, moving my hair, tickling my shoulders, the breeze that, when I closed my eyes, made me a child again, that breeze has left, and I still cannot smell the snow.

"Is everything alright?" asks Ryan as he walks through the door.

"Yeah. I just needed a minute. That's all. I was smelling the wind, and it made me remember you."

"It's odd, the things a memory hides, isn't it?"

"It is."

Ryan comes over to the side of the bed, sits down next to me and throws his legs up.

"I'm sorry if this is weird with her being here."

"It's fine," I say as I reach over on the nightstand and grab an envelope. "Here. Take this and read it later."

"Not now?"

"No."

"Okay," he says and puts it into his pocket. "I'll keep it with the other one."

"I can't believe you still have it," I say as he takes it out and shows me the letter I wrote one September morning while Toto chased the late mayflies. "It's just about that thing we talked about."

"Me killing you?"

"It's a poem about you and me, and then there's one more little request to help calm my nerves."

"Claire. Ryan. Dinner's ready," Mom calls from downstairs.

"You were supposed to cook dinner tonight. You pawned it off on Mom, didn't you?"

"She didn't trust me with the stove, said she'd have to watch me, so I didn't burn the place down. I told her to cook the whole goddamned thing then."

"What about Nicole?"

"She got a text from work and had to leave."

"Let's go," I say and get off the bed.

"Is your appetite back?" he asks as he sets his feet on the floor.

"No, and I'm starting to look pregnant because of this stupid organ." I prod my swollen belly with my fingers. "It's my timer."

"You are absolutely beautiful," he says, walks over and holds me."

"So are you," I say. "Maybe I'll eat a blueberry pancake, just because you didn't make it."

"Get on," he says as he crouches. "I'll give you a piggyback."

"You know who doesn't like piggybacks?" I ask.

"Who?"

"Nobody in the history of the world," I say and leap onto his back, wrapping my arms around his neck and my legs around his hips.

"Hold on tight," he says as he skips out of my room, down the hallway and to the stairs.

Mom's already got our plates in the living room, and the television's turned to Jeopardy.

"The River Ouse," I say.

"What is the River Ouse," says a professor from Ithaca.

"Finns," says Mom.

"No, it's The White Horse Pub," I say.

"What is The White Horse Pub," says the professor again.

"There's no use in playing against you," Mom says.

"Fuck no," says Ryan. "How do you know everything, ever?"

"I know because of KRS-One," I say.

"I love that song," he says, and I smile because he understands.

"Pass the syrup," says Mom.

"Heptonstall," I say.

"What is Heptonstall Church," echoes the garbage man from New York City.

"Ketchum," says Mom, as Trebek gives the answer.

"Good one, Mom."

"You're both nerds," Ryan claims.

Once Jeopardy's over, Mom puts on Titanic, and once Mr. Dawson disappears, so does Mom.

"Good night my babies," she says.

"Night, Mom," we say.

I take the blanket off the back of the couch and lay it over our laps, tuck my knees up to my chest and lean into him.

"What now?" he asks.

"Let's watch Message in a Bottle."

"I saw that movie in the theater," he says proudly and puts his hand on my thigh, making me instantly regret wearing jeans. "I'll go put it in."

He gets up and searches the DVD tower for the movie then puts it in the player. I take the remote, turn up the volume then lift the blanket for him when he comes back.

"What happened to your pants?" he asks as he puts his hand on my thigh and searches with his fingers.

"I'm not sure. Maybe you should keep looking," I say.

I lean back and stretch out on the couch while Ryan continues looking for my pants, and I for his.

The Milky Way whirls behind my lids. The incoming tide drops wave upon wave onto my shore. I open my eyes long enough to see Nicole in the doorway. Her eyes see mine, and I don't move anyway Ryan doesn't make me.

I press my fingertips onto my eyes, release my head and later, when our pants are found, but not worn, and Ryan lays next to me, she is no longer in the doorway.

We don't speak, Ryan and I, but listen to the breathing while waiting for our hearts to allay.

"Ryan," I say, "let's stay up all night and just before the sun comes up, go to River Pond and watch it rise. I have an extra pair of snowshoes for you."

"I'll put on the coffee," he says.

"I'll get the cups."

65

Ryan

Ten in the morning and I wake up playing pantsless Twister with Claire.

I watch as her eyes open for the first time today. She smiles, closes them again, puts her hand on my chest.

"I guess we missed the sunrise," she says while tugging the blanket to her chin.

"We can go now," I say.

"Nonsense. We're going shopping. We can go another time."

"Shopping for what?"

"Let's dress up for the Supremes concert," she says.

"Dress up? Like what?" I ask.

"I don't know. We'll find something. Pass my pants, will you?"

"Coffee's ready, you two," Sylvia calls from the kitchen. "French toast is on the way."

"Where are my pants?" I ask.

"I don't know," she says.

"There they are. How did they get over there?" I say and fetch them.

"You must have given them a mighty toss," she says and catches the pants and shirt I throw.

"A mighty toss?"

"Mighty Ryan, how's my hair?" she asks as I pull down my shirt.

"Hot," I say then walk into the kitchen.

"Here you go," Sylvia says and puts a full plate in front of each of us. "What are your plans for today?"

"Clothes shopping," Claire says. "I'm going to dress Ryan up for the concert.

"Concert?" asks Sylvia.

"The Supremes cover band we talked about last night. Remember?" Claire asks.

"I do now."

"You want to come with us, Mom?"

"No, that's alright. I'm going to kick around here and hopefully finish Anna Karenina. You two have fun, though," she says. "Try to eat something, honey."

Claire puts the untouched plate of food on the floor for Toto.

"I'll get her stoned," I tell Sylvia. "Then I'll drive by a Taco Bell."

"I need to brush my teeth, then we should go," she says.

"I need to brush mine, too. Can I use yours?" I ask.

"Sure."

"Gross," Sylvia says.

"It's hot.".

"Come on, boy," Claire says and wraps her palm around my thumb.

I follow her upstairs to the bathroom where we share a blue toothbrush, and she spritzes cucumber melon body spray on both of us.

"That's what Mom calls a whore's bath," she says.

"Your mom's mean."

"Shush. Let's go."

It's a warm morning, about fifty. The snow's on its way out, and so are we. I get in the car, roll down the window and light a cigarette as we slip and slide down Ruby Lane and turn onto Route 1.

"Did you open the envelope I gave you?" she asks.

"Not yet," I say and reach into my pants pocket. "It's gone. They're both gone."

"What? How?"

"I don't have it. My pockets are empty."

"Maybe it's on the floor beside the couch. That's fine, I guess. Mom won't read it if it has your name on it."

"What did it say?" I ask.

"I guess I can say it out loud. I just don't want Mom to find out."

"Promise," I say.

"I wrote a poem for you when I was daydreaming about us being old together. You know that."

"I've got to find it."

"One more thing. I may have also asked you to shoot me," she says.

"What?"

"I don't want to take any chances of not dying. I'll never let Mom see me suffer. That's the only way to make sure."

"Shooting you up is one thing, but shooting you is another. There's no goddamn way."

"What's the difference?"

"The needless destruction of beauty," I say.

"Isn't that life's job, though?" she asks. "God's purpose?"

"The body belongs to Satan," I correct.

"Makes sense."

"I guess your real beauty will already be gone."

"Feel this." Claire takes my hand and sets it on her stomach. "This is the beginning of my death, my body killing itself."

"Why do you need me to pull the trigger?"

"I want to be sleeping. I want the pills to knock me out first," she says. "It's a perfect death."

"I can't," I say, and that's the last sentence until we get on the interstate in Brewer, and I remember my promise to Sylvia.

"Want a coffee?" I ask.

"How many people have you killed?"

"Why would you ask that?"

"I'm dying to know."

"That's good stuff."

"Because my life is null, and I want to know everything I can."

She holds my hand.

"Three," I tell her.

"What's one more then?" she asks without a hint of fear.

"They were terrible people. I never went looking. They found me," I explain.

She pulls off the interstate, onto Broadway and into the greasy, fried smell of cheap Chinese food.

"I found you, too," she tells me. "I may not be terrible, but this disease is. I saw my grandmother die terribly. Mom will never see me like that.

"Why are you taking me to the mall?" I ask, changing the subject.

She knows what I'm doing, laughs, then plays along.

"We're clothes shopping."

"What am I? At the mall?"

"At the Salvation Army. In the back. Dick."

"Weird," I say.

"What is?"

"Hiding salvation."

"It's not hidden. It's just around the back," she explains. "Besides, where else are we going to find a fedora and a poodle skirt?"

"Right next to the vintage checkered slacks some guy shit in before he died."

"Gross," she says.

"That's what I'm saying."

She parks in front of a red concrete building with a massive sheet of snow on its roof. We get out, cautiously walk under the awning and into the store.

"Hey," says a chubby woman with a mole on her lip the size of a used eraser.

Claire and I walk up and down aisles that smell like an attic.

"Told you," she says. "A poodle skirt and look, over there on the wall. Here, hold these."

She passes me two pin-striped suits.

"When did you pick these up?" I ask, but she's already at the wall.

"A fedora," I say, as I creep closer with an armload of style.

"Two of them. Dealer's choice," she says.

"I like the white one."

"I like the black one."

"Me too."

She picks the black hat off the wall, and we go to the dressing room. Claire holds the door open for me, looks around for the mole, then hurries in.

"Might as well have some fun before the day's over," she says.

"Your hair smells like strawberries.".

Twenty minutes and a broken mirror later, we're paying for two suits, a hat, a gray and pink poodle skirt and a tight white blouse.

"Are you sure your Mom won't read the letter where you're asking me to shoot you?" I ask and finish with a laugh, which carries over into her words.

"There's also a poem, remember?"

"Hope so."

Claire shoves her hands into two tight jean pockets and puts a twenty on the table in front of the cashier.

"Would you like to donate the remainder to the Salvation Army?" asks the cashier.

"I would not like to pay for salvation," I say.

"Ryan. Stop. Keep it," Claire says.

"Why don't you give them your car, too," I say.

"Where will I do you on the ride home then?"

"We're not giving you the car, be happy with the two dollars and eighty-two cents," I say to the cashier, who's already back to her Knitter's World.

"See you around," Claire says as we walk out.

"You're quite the gentleman," I tell her as she opens the car door for me.

"Why, thank you, mister."

Once we're in the car, Claire puts on a Lana Del Rey album, turns it on low and the ride into downtown's as smooth as the music.

"Where are we going?" I ask.

"I'm not sure. I just want to take the long way there."

Claire's phone rings.

"It's Mom," she says. "Here, answer it. I'm not driving and talking."

"You're such a role model."

"I'm a road model."

"Hey," I say into the phone.

"Ryan, where are you guys?"

"Just left downtown Bangor. We're around Winterport. What's up?

"Claire's driving, isn't she?"

"She is."

"Ask her if she found the envelope," says Claire.

"Did you find a mauve envelope on the living room floor?" I ask.

"Are you sure it's not salmon or blush?"

"If mauve and salmon had a baby and named it lavender."

"No. I haven't seen anything."

"Can you check under the couch, maybe in the cushions," I ask.

"Hold on."

"Anything?"

"Nothing," she says. "Just one of Claire's books."

"Fuck," I say.

"Eff," says Claire.

"We'll be home in an hour, or so."

"Okay. Bye bye."

"Baby, bye bye bye," I sing then hang up. "So, good news and not so good news."

"I heard everything. Mom talks wicked loud. Did she say which book she found?"

"Nope."

"I bet it's E.E. Cummings. I lost that awhile back when I had the flu.

"When we get home, do you want to put on a thick coat and a winter hat, go up to River Pond, and dance a jig on your favorite rock," I ask.

"Today?"

"Why not?"

Claire coughs, and I see that her skin is flushed red.

"It's so hot in here," she says and rolls down the window.

I grab her hand.

"You're hot."

"It's a fever. I've been getting them a lot" She pulls over. "You need to drive. I'm having a hard time seeing the road."

She doesn't say anything the whole ride back. Not as we cross the scarily high bridge connecting Prospect to Bucksport. Not as we turn onto Ruby Lane, and not as I help

her so she doesn't slip on the wet snow
that's quickly turning to ice.

"You need to go to the hospital,
honey," Sylvia says as we go into the house
and toward the stairs.

"I'm fine. I just need help to bed, so
I can rest."

I take her hand, put my other arm
around her waist and help her up the steps.

"It sounds like you have something in
your lungs," Sylvia calls from the bottom of
the stairs. "I'm calling an ambulance."
"They can't cure the inevitable. I just need
to lay down."

Once we make it to Claire's room, she
lays in bed, and I open the two windows
above the headboard.

"Oh, that breeze feels nice. I'm so
glad it cooled off," she says.

"It's freezing out."

"Will you pass me that cup of water?"
she asks while pointing at the nightstand.
"And the pill bottle."

"Eighties, huh?" I say and hand her the
bottle.

"Is that good?" she asks.

"They're strong."

"Pass me four," she says.

"Four? Jesus, that would kill me," I
say.

"I'm tougher than you, mon petit pissenlit" she says.

"Je T'aime,' I say. "I'm going to double check for the letter, then you're going to get a fresh cup of water. How long has that glass been there?"

There's this look that pretty, innocent girls get when they get real high. Their skin becomes soft, warm like your favorite blanket when your toes get cold. Her eyes widen, becoming observers rather than judgers, child-like rather than adult-like. Her motions are lazy, tired, playful like her messy hair and goofy smile. Anything can make her happy now because life gets no better than when you're fucked on opiates.

I go to her dresser, open drawers until I find the one with the comfortable clothes and take out a soft pair of pajama bottoms and a Rihanna concert shirt.

"I saw her when she came to San Fran," I say. "One of the best shows I ever saw.

"Numb," she says with wet, smiling lips.

"My favorite."

"I heard you singing it one day at River Pond."

She sees me bringing the clothes over and unhooks her belt then pushes off the jeans.

216

"Give me," she says and sticks out her fingers to catch the pajamas.

She pulls them on in one smooth motion then takes off her T-shirt, folding it and setting it on the nightstand.

"Hurry. The wind is cold," she says. "It feels perfect, though."

"You should have worn a bra, then, huh?" I say as I hold the shirt.

She sticks out her fingers again, stretching.

"Come on. Come on. Come on. I'm freezing."

"Here you go, but I give to thee with complete regret. You are much too perfect to be covered with mortal clothing."

"You're so sweet, dildo," she says as she pulls the T-shirt over her head, and my eyes follow the bottom hem down until it covers all of her except a half-inch of soft flesh above the blue waistband.

"Everybody get dressed. I'm coming up," Sylvia calls.

"Mom! I missed you," she says as Sylvia stands in the doorway.

"Missed you too, honey."

"You got a joint, Sylvia?"

"It's hard watching her high, isn't it?" she asks as she places a hand on the needle bumps on my forearm. "Her father was

217

the same as you. Here's a two-paper joint. Enjoy it and try to forget about this other stuff, okay?"

"I wish you were my mom."

"Me too, but only in the way that you didn't sleep with your sister last night."

"Hey. How'd you know about that?" Claire asks as she throws her legs off the bed and stumbles across the room to Sylvia.

"Sex is not quiet, and sex on drugs is certainly not."

"A lot of fun, though," I say.

"Obviously," Claire agrees.

"Okay. That's enough. I'm still your mother."

"For a few weeks, anyway," says Claire, and then she sucks in a breath, looking as if she understands that even though she's taken enough pills to tame Satan, she's just said something that never should have been said. She stands up. "Sorry, Mom. I'm so sorry. I didn't mean to say it like that."

"I know, honey. This is an impossible situation. Completely, totally, utterly impossible."

Claire takes two steps back and falls to the bed, looks up at the cracks forming in the ceiling paint and speaks.

"How do you stand on the track, seeing the train coming from yesterday, knowing that neither of you can move, and continue to be thankful for each breath? As soon as you see the train, that one monstrous headlight like God's eye, and hear that whistle blow as powerful as any storm, each breath from then on is only demon laughter." She stretches out her legs and begins to make snow angels on the comforter. "Stupid, stupid world."

"Are you going to light that?" asks Sylvia as she points to the blunt hanging from my lips. "I'm going to need it to be on the same level as her."

I shut the bedroom door and kill the lights while Claire puts on Rihanna's Anti then turns the volume up, so it's no longer easy to talk but simple to feel the push of the bass. We clam bake until Sylvia and I lay beside Claire, searching a ceiling lit only by the light reflecting off the moon reflecting off the snow.

"I've wanted to go see Pollen," Claire says between songs, "but I don't anymore."

"Why?" Sylvia asks.

"She's exactly where she needs to be. I fear I'll never see my beautiful rock in the pond again, though."

"Do you want to go up tomorrow?"

"There's way too much snow."

"Right."

"Do you mind if I paint on your wall?"
I ask Claire.

"Not at all. I wish you would."

"Can I borrow your car and a couple bucks?" I ask.

"Keys and the money are in my jeans," she says.

"Be back in an hour, Mon petite pee lint."

"Pissenlint," she corrects. "Oh, and don't forget to look for the letter down there."

"I told you, it's not there," says Sylvia. "I turned every cushion. I found the book you lost, *95 Poems*."

"My favorite book," says Claire.

"You say that about every book."

"And I've never lied."

66
Claire

EE Cummings wrote: So,when kiss Spring comes we'll kiss each kiss other on kiss the kiss lips because tic clocks toc don't make a toctic difference to kisskiss you and to kiss me).

Like all poetry, this is a puzzle. Some are figured out while most never are. It's singular, lonely, understood differently by the writer than by the reader, but as I lay on the couch tossing the words around my brain, the television droning, the sun so bright looking out the window is unbearable, I think I understand. If Ryan and I were to have a joint eulogy, I would want those words to be the only ones read; there has never been a prettier string of words strung together that sum up all of life's enjoyment as succinctly as those, in a roundabout way.

Mom comes in and sits in a wooden rocking chair by the bright window and blocks the sun for me.

"How are you feeling, honey?" she asks as she opens Anna Karenina.

"Fine. Are you almost done with that book?"

"It's a million pages, but I'm almost there. The book is phenomenal, but it's like Atlas Shrugged. Is it necessary? Does your book have to be longer than the Bible? Even the Bible doesn't have to be that long."

"I know, right? Jesus was born. You go to heaven," I say as I take another pill and fall into the crack between the cushions and the backrest. "Is Ryan almost done up there?"

"I think so. He hasn't slept all night."

"I guess I slept enough for the both of us," I say as I push through this concrete life to sit up and put my feet on the floor.

Mom lights a joint, and I walk over to her and look out the window. The sun has finally moved enough so the sky above Ryan's house appears bluer than it probably should. It's not really his home, though, as he's been staying with me every night. Mom walks around the room, leaving a stream of gray smoke from the joint as she circles the room, taking a puff at each window until she's next to me again.

"I need to take a bath," I say. "I feel dirty."

Mom hugs me.

"You're warm, and you smell fine," she says.

"Delicious, even," says Ryan as he enters the living room.

"Where did you come from?" I ask.

"Straight outta Compton."

"You mean San Francisco, poser?"

"Right. Let's go," he says then scoops me up.

I hook my arm around his shoulder and feel the vibrations of his voice as he carries me into the paint fumes. My nose has gotten used to it since Ryan got back from the store last night with four gallons, but it's strong up here, and as he takes me into my bedroom, I pay no attention, but stick my nose onto his collar and inhale the fabric sheet smell of his hoodie.

"It's absolutely amazing," I say as I stand in front of a wall-to-wall painting of River Pond. "You even did it so I'm looking out from my rock."

"You can always see anything one more time," he says as he puts me down on the bed and sits next to me.

"How did you do all this in one night?"

"Coffee and weed," he says. "Actually, I was stone cold sober."

"I love you, Ryan Alexander."

He doesn't look at me, but at the analog clock on the nightstand because he's crying. I can tell by the way the corner of

223

his cheek twitches, by the way he fights to keep the edge of his lips steady.

"I don't want to live without you," he says.

"Don't say that."

"I was dead before you, and I'll be dead after."

"I love you too much to let you become a cliche'," I say, and this makes him laugh. "That would be the biggest tragedy of all, to have something so wonderful be made null by a lame-ass move. You're the essence of cool."

"The birth of cool."

"...and you are much too cool for that," I remind him.

"Then what do I do?"

"What do you love to do?"

"Drugs," he says.

"Is that all?"

"I paint."

"Then be a painter. Don't suffocate, just do whatever you want and don't hurry death."

"Everything else will only be a child's drawing of the original model. Without you, I go back to black and white television, cassettes, hand-written letters, Christopher Pike, Bon Jovi, Goosebumps, En Vogue.

"Irrelevant, but awesome?" I say.

224

"Paled by experience."

"I'm going to take a bath. Thank you so much for this painting."

I try to get out of bed but can only suck in hollow breaths. I lay down, stretch my hands over my head, huff in anger, laugh, mess my hair, smile like a child that's been given soda and a sugary slice of pecan pie.

"Ryan, let's buy a gun."

67
Claire

Behind a long display case stands a man with gray hair curling out above his ears, a tucked in t-shirt, and a smile that warmed this room the moment we walked in.

"Anything you need, just holler."

"Thank you," I say.

"I'll just leave you be, then. Let me know when you want something," he says then opens a book.

"What are you reading," I ask, and this makes him smile.

"Fishing stories. I once got to striper fish with the writer. He got skunked, but I got a thirty-pounder." He nods up to a monstrous silver fish on the wall behind him. "There she is."

"Was that a good day?" I ask.

"One of the best," he says with a smile.

"I bet that would make a good story."

The man holds up the book.

"Pages twenty-two to eighty-two," he says, and goes back to reading.

I walk to the end of the display case, as far away from this sweet old man as I can get.

"Which one?" I ask.

"I don't know. I can't think," Ryan says.

"What did you use?"

He studies the wall rack behind the case and points to a shotgun.

"Gross," I say. "I want something down here, something small. It's got to fit in my hand."

"How can you do this to yourself?"

226

"Ryan, the train's close. It's not a question of acceptance at this point. It just is," I say and lean back to get a better view of the gun case. "It's liberating to know I don't have to suffer, and also that this stupid universe gave me a helper."

There are no words as gloss protects his eyes. I look down through my reflection in the glass display case, to the machinated bottle that'll hold my final pill. Each barrel is different. Some are blue, some are silver, some are rusted, but all shine from a coating of oil. I want to touch them all, to know how they'll feel pressed against me. Will it be cold? Will it be warmed by Ryan's grip?

"Do you think he'd let me try them on?" I ask. "You know, to see which one fits my temple the best."

"I fit your temple the best," he says.

"That's the one."

I choose an old-fashioned thing, something real sexy, a revolver with a wooden handle, then I interrupt the owner reading his book.

".357 Ruger," he says. "Good choice for personal protection."

"Do you ever read that book?" I ask as I point to the Bible behind the register.

227

"Mostly from a distance. When I need to read it, I just think about what the Lord would say about whatever's ailing me. A reminder is all that it is."

"Of what?"

"Just that it's there when I need it. Hopefully not for a few more years."

The man opens the revolver, spins the wheel and inspects each hole.

"Thank you for checking. I don't accidentally want to shoot myself."

"No, you don't," he says. "What kind of load do you prefer?"

"Excuse me?" I say, and this makes him blush, which makes us laugh.

"Bullets, ma'am. Bullets."

"Right. Bullets. Whatever will keep me safe."

He bends and slides open a stubborn door below the display, pulls out a shoebox and sets a case of bullets on the counter.

"These ought to do just fine," he says. "That's what I use."

"Then that's what I'll use."

After paying, we're warned about a nor'easter that's supposed to make the last snowstorm, which totaled three feet, look like a "California rainstorm". I thank the man for the warning, promise to tell my mother, then Ryan and I walk under a

228

jingling bell as we open the door to a white town patched with piles of dirty snowbanks.

"What happened to Nicole?" I ask while tightening my scarf.

"I don't know. I haven't seen her since blueberry pancake night," he says, and I instantly know what happened to the envelope."

"That bitch."

68
Ryan

Claire's driving us home at a hundred miles an hour. No cars are on the road, just us and the potholes hiding under the gravelly snow.

"You did what?" I ask.

"Let her watch."

"And you didn't do anything?"

"Nope."

"You're a savage," I say and slip two fingers inside her jeans pocket and take out the cell phone.

"I could have gotten it for you," she says, taking her eyes off the road and killing me with them.

"Don't be boring."

I punch in Nicole's number.

"Hello?"

"Hey. It's Ryan."

I light a cigarette.

"I was wondering how long it would take you to realize the letters were gone," she says. "I had to get back at her somehow for looking at me like that."

"I'm surprised she could keep her eyes open," I say, and Claire slaps my arm.

"What is that supposed to mean?"

"Did you open them?"

"No, but I'm pulling into the post office now. I went home. Sorry about all of this. I've never been this petty. Friends?"

"Friends," I say.

"Thank you. I'll talk to you later."

"Make sure to send the letters."

"I'll overnight them right now. I'll see you if you ever come back to San Francisco."

Nicole hangs up.

"What's she going to do with them?" asks Claire.

"She's at the post office right now."

"Do you believe her?"

"I do."

"Then I do, too. I should have just talked to you about it."

"I want to read the poem."

"I want you to, too."

We make it home in ten minutes, but Claire drives so slow up Ruby Lane that it takes that much time again to make it to where we are.

"Have you even touched the gas pedal?" I ask, putting my hand on her thigh and feeling the muscle tighten.

She cocks her head and looks at me so a long curl falls from behind her ear and rests on the curve above her breast.

"Are you in a hurry?" she asks.

"Fuck no. Put it in reverse."

"Not a chance," she says and nudges the snow bank with the bumper, picks my hand up from her leg and presses her lips onto my knuckles. "Let's walk the rest of the way while I've got the strength to do so. We can come back and get the car in the morning."

"To do so, we shall."

69
Claire

"You look like Clyde," I say while adjusting his collar.

231

"You look like Bonnie."

"Ready?"

"Ready."

We leave my bedroom and go downstairs.

"You two are adorable," Mom says while waiting at the door.

"Are you ready?" I ask her.

"I think I'm going to stay in for the night. You two go. I'm on the last fifty pages of Anna Karenina, and I have got to finish."

I grab Ryan's hand and squeeze.

"We'd love for you to come," I tell her.

"Nobody remembers anybody else from the Barrow gang, anyway. You two have fun."

"Okay. See you tonight."

"Check it, Sylvia," says Ryan as he bends down and kisses her cheek.

"Aren't you sweet."

She steps back, opens the door, and we leave.

To drive down Ruby Lane as the sun sets is to drive through a tunnel. Even though the tree branches above have lost all their leaves, the branches are still so tightly knit they reflect my headlights and create a bright ceiling where the details of the viney branches, which would otherwise be hidden within the evening's fading light, are shown to be woven as tightly as any weaver's basket. When I turn onto Route 1 and look up at a sky that's a minute too early for the first star, I become minute.

"There's a lot of people here," I say while turning into the Grange.

"Read that mother 'effin sign," says Ryan. "We've got to go."

"Who's Robert Lancing? And why do I care that this is a benefit concert for him?"

"He's my Ocean Side friend, Bobby Lancing," he says, and I shut the car off. "What are you doing?"

"We didn't get dressed for nothing," I say. "Come on."

"God, you're dark."

We get out of the car and walk toward a group of down-faced people standing around a keg.

"Sorry about your friend," I say.

"Aren't you two a blast from the past, real good-looking couple."

"God damn shame," says a guy still staring at the ground, his hands stuffed into jean pockets and a cigarette dangling from his mouth. "I'll miss my brother."

"We just came for the concert. We don't mean to intrude, just wanted to offer our condolences."

"What happened to him?" Ryan asks.

"Suicide."

"Shot himself, upset he couldn't support his family, then drove off, and we've never seen him since."

"He only left a note for the boss."

"Why his boss?"

"He's our father, too. That's just what we always called him around work, the boss."

"We're trying to raise a little money for Bobby's family," explains the man next his brother.

"We hope the best for the Lancings. I hear they were a loving, charitable family," Ryan says.

"Never hurt a fly," his brother tell us.

"A saint, if I ever met one. We'll just be out back on the pier. Ready, Claire?"

I hand twenty-two dollars to Bobby's hundred-and-twenty pound brother. He stuffs it in his pocket, and Ryan hands him some change.

"Here's eighty-two cents. It's all I have."

"Good night for being on the dock," says a man as he pumps the keg. "It's a little chilly, but it'll be good to stretch your legs before we're all buried in the snow."

"Some say five feet over the weekend."

We leave the gravel parking lot, pull our coats a little tighter and step onto the shoveled path leading to the dock.

"Why did they say suicide?" he asks as we step onto the icy pier. "Watch your step."

I think for a moment while looking between the cracks to the sloshing ocean below, which I can't see, but only hear.

"Insurance, maybe? They probably didn't want to pay out for an accidental death."

"I bet you're right. You're always right, aren't you?" he asks while waves slowly roll by. "Look, the first star's out."

"That's Venus," I tell him.

"I always wanted to see her with you."

Ryan takes my hand, and we look in opposite directions until we get to the end of the dock. A gray, wooden bench rests opposite a swing set.

"May I have the first swing," he asks while holding out the rubber seat.

"And the last."

I sit down under an early moon, whose light spreads like butter across the ocean.

The sounds of the Supremes fills the harbor, and Ryan sits in the swing next to me.

"What now?" he asks and lights a cigarette.

"Now we enjoy the concert. These are the best seats in the house."

"That they are, my dear. That they are."

Cigarette smoke hovers over the pier, fifteen, or so feet above the cold water, and we lazily pump our legs, rocking slowly to imitate the waves.

70
Claire

Ryan clasps my hand as we crest the final hill after finishing an evening stroll on Ruby Lane.

"The concert last night was pretty great," he says.

"That it was," I say just as a deer skips across the road.

"I didn't think we'd make it before dark."

"I never worried," I say and take his warm hand in mine. "It's pretty how the setting sun can turn the snow pink."

He let's go of my hand and runs his down my spine, lifts my sweater and places his palm on the top of my belt.

"Toto, where have you been?" I ask as he sprints down the road.

"Mackin' on hoes," Ryan says.

Toto leaps into my arms, splattering me with dirty snow, and I carry him like a baby up the road and into the house.

Mom sits at the kitchen table reading her book. She raises a finger to tell us it'll be a moment before she can talk. She puts it down then proclaims "I've finished this goddamn book. Boy, was it long," she says.

"Would you do it again?" I ask.

"I'd choose a shorter one."

"Mom, I've got a little request. A teeny, miniature thing, really."

"What is it, my dear?"

"Is there any way Ryan and I can have the house for the night?"

"You know, so we can watch Netflix and hang out," he says.

"Netflix?" I ask.

"He means an excuse to make love, my dear."

"Oh."

"Of course, I will. Toto and I can stay at Ryan's. Is that alright with you?" she asks him.

"It's your house. I wasn't messing when I said that. I don't want it. You bought it."

"You can't be serious," she says.

"Just let me crash there when I want, which I'll probably never need to. That's all I care about. It's way more than a hobo needs" he says.

I loop my arm around Ryan's and lean my head on his bicep.

"What does a hobo need?" Mom asks.

"Just a petal to catch the dew," I say.

"Is that all?" asks Sylvia. "Will a petal keep you dry during this next storm?"

"I'm afraid that's what your house is for."

"Silly, stupid, stupid trials and tribulations," I say as Mom lights a bowl and passes it to Ryan.

He takes a slow hit then hands it to me.

"Why are you crying, sweetheart?" Mom asks me.

"I'm just going to miss you. So, so much."

"I'll be back tomorrow."

"I know you will," I say, walk over, wrap my arms around her neck and bury my face into her shoulder. I feel Toto's paw tapping my toes.

"It's almost dark. I should get going. Ryan, I might need you to help dig me out tomorrow; the nor'easter's supposed to hit in the morning," she says and loosens her grip, but I can't let go, not yet. Just one more second, two more. I drop my arms and step away. "Ryan, this letter came for you today from Nicole. You should get a permanent address."

"There's no such thing," he says.

"It's my letter," I remind him. "Wait to open it, okay?"

"When?"

"Before the snow falls."

71
Claire

Mom and Toto walk down the path in the snow connecting my front porch to Ryan's back porch. Once Mom reaches the house, she turns around, probably lost in the angelicness of Apple Ridge; this time of evening, just before night when the sun's already below the horizon but some sneaky shades of violet and red deconstruct into yellow then gray, it becomes breathtaking to get lost in the colors igniting the sky above us.

"You can see it again tomorrow night, you, Ryan and Toto," I say as the vapor of my words vanishes from the kitchen window.

I stand still, looking down the mountain as Mom goes inside and, a few minutes later, see smoke billowing from the chimney. I take Ryan's hand and we climb the stairs.

When I was a kid and Mom and I were driving up from Georgia to visit Gram on summer vacation, the same summer I met Ryan, we stopped at Storyland to ride the roller coaster. I remember it perfectly; the weather was absolutely marvelous.

My hair wasn't so much flung by the wind, as it was brushed, like the way Mom did while we waited in line and ate sticky cotton candy. My skin and clothes weren't bothered by the breeze, but caressed by it the way Mom stroked my hair as we inched closer to the gate.

I couldn't smell french fries or dough boys, or the cigarettes people were allowed to smoke in public back then, but it was the smell of a muddy field, of hot rocks beneath tiny bare feet, of hotdog wrappers marred with globs of sunbaked ketchup and the flies circling them like vultures. I wasn't so much above them as I am now, but could kneel without disturbing them and be eye-level with the bugs and the ten or so strands of grass poking through a mound of brown dirt. Somewhere on my journey from down there to up here, I'd forgotten about them until just now. It's funny, these things you remember.

Once it was our turn and we stepped into the red shuttle, we we're locked in by a man I thought had the greatest job in the world; imagine the happiness he brought into this world. If Ryan were with us back then, he would have said the man was the greatest hobo ever to have lived.

I became scared when the chains and gears started to grind, the carriage beginning to creep uphill slower than those strolling into the Bingo tent next door.

"It's okay, little Claire Bear. I'll keep you safe," Mom said, sensing my fear, and when she put her arm around my shoulder and pressed her cheek onto the top of my head, I knew she was telling the truth.

At least once a summer, somewhere along a walk to nowhere in particular, I'm gifted with that bouquet again, and with it, the

241

smile of the little barefoot girl who had just turned five that day at 8:22 a.m while standing in line for a roller coaster, who, the very next morning, would quietly stand beside a tire swing with the love of her life as the sun rose above Apple Ridge while her mother snapped pictures of them.

As I lay down in bed and set the empty pill bottle on the nightstand, I take a sip of fresh water Ryan hands to me.

"Promise me you'll take care of Mom. Don't let her see any of this."

"I promise."

I take one more look at the mural on the wall of River Pond, then close my eyes, put out my palm and smile as he places his on top.

I drift down into the bed. Further and further. I think to open the windows, to let in new air, but I can't speak, let alone move. Early winter wind slides down my cheek as Ryan presses on the bed and opens the windows.

That little spot in my brain, the part where the "I" resides, grows fuzzy at the edges and collapses into itself. He breathes. Loudly. In and out. In and out. It's all I can listen to as it becomes the sound of August waves erasing sand castles.

There's a pressing on my temple, like
the pad of an index finger, and I consider
doing whatever I can to postpone what is
about to happen, but I hear the click of the
gear and understand this ride is rolling
forward. In a breath, maybe two, it'll be
over, and I can plant my bare feet in the
hot dirt again and watch flies eating
ketchup.
    "I haven't changed a bit," he says;
but we have

72
Ryan

Mr. Alexander,
    I have written this fairy tale about an
older you and me. It's called Before the Snow
Falls.

Replace the barn, Ryan.
It's crumbling and weak.
The roof has buckled
From too much snow.

The floor boards sag
And the trusses do, too.
One more storm and come
spring, it'll be in the dirt.

243

Claire, we built that barn
from my father's plans,
on the rich soil of your mother's land,
And what it's produced
Has served us well.

Sure, the crow's feet scratched the windows,
and the left side leans with a limp.
We can replace the sill,
but you're right, by next storm, it's over.

It's much too much for only one.
We can do it together,
You and me,
As soon as our pills are popped
with the bitter juice of prunes.

I promise, Claire, this time
We'll build it with brick,
(The best we can find)
And the walls will last
Twenty-two lifetimes.

I know we will, my pissenlint,
But please, we must hurry to remove the nails
before the snow falls
And it's buried for the rest of winter.

Mr. Alexander,

I love you.
p.s.
Please shoot me, too.

(We'll talk later.)
        xoxox

A message from the author's friend

To the person at the other end of the line,
holding the hollow tin can,
I apologize for the absentee.

After hitching around with a fishbowl
of Frisco snowballs
and a handful of vanilla microdots,
Michael James arrived in Maine
a sullen schema,
speaking only to a 486 and me,
Abigail S. Pea.
The novel's title aside,
(and a few minor things)
Before the Snow Falls arrives
unadulterated in your hand.

So, even though Michael couldn't be here,
He sends his single regard.
I publish this for Michael,
a good friend of mine.

Literally yours,

-Abigail Pea